INDIAN IDYLLS

Translated from the Hindi by

Edwin Arnold

First published in 1907

Published by Left of Brain Books

Copyright © 2023 Left of Brain Books

ISBN 978-1-396-32508-3

First Edition

PUBLISHER'S PREFACE

About the Book

"Indian Idylls. Sir Edwin Arnold, translator. More stories from the Mahabharata, rendered in poetry."

(Quote from sacred-texts.com)

CONTENTS

PREFACE

SOME time ago I wrote and published, in a paper entitled "The Iliad and Odyssey of India," the following passages:-

"There exist two colossal, two unparalleled, epic poems in the sacred language of India, -the Mahâbhârata and the Râmâyana, -which were not known to Europe, even by name, until Sir William Jones announced their existence; and one of which, the larger, since his time, has been made public only by fragments, by mere specimens, hearing to those vast treasures of Sanskrit literature such small proportion as cabinet samples of ore have to the riches of a mine. Yet these most remarkable poems contain almost all the history of ancient India, so far as it can be recovered; together with such inexhaustible details of its political, social, and religious life, that the antique Hindu world really stands epitomized in them. The Old Testament is not more interwoven with the Jewish race, nor the New Testament with the civilization of Christendom, nor the Koran with the records and destinies of Islam, than are these two Sanskrit poems with that unchanging and teeming Population which Her Majesty, Queen Victoria, rules as Empress of Hindustan. The stories, songs, and ballads; the histories and genealogies; the nursery tales and religious discourses; the art; the learning, the philosophy, the creeds, the moralities, the modes of thought, the very phrases, saying, turns of expression, and daily ideas of the Hindu people are taken from these poems. Their children and their wives are named out of them; so are their cities, temples, streets, and cattle. They have constituted the library, the newspaper, and the Bible-generation after generation-for all the succeeding and countless millions of Indian people; and it replaces patriotism with that race, and, stands in stead of nationality, to possess these two precious and inexhaustible books, and to drink from them as from mighty and overflowing rivers. The value ascribed in Hindustan to these too little known epics has transcended all literary standards established in the West. They are personified, worshipped, and cited as being something divine. To read or even listen to them is thought by the devout Hindu sufficiently meritorious to bring prosperity to his household here, and happiness in the next world; they are held also to give wealth to the poor, health to the sick, wisdom to the ignorant; and the recitation of certain parvas and shlokas in them can fill the household of the barren, it is believed, with children. A concluding passage of the great poem says:-

"'The reading of this Mahâbhârata destroys all sin and produces virtue; so much so, that the pronunciation of a single shloka is sufficient to wipe away much guilt. This Mahâbhârata contains the history of the gods, of the Rishis in heaven and those on earth, of the Gandharvas and the Rákshasas. It also contains the life and actions of the one God, holy, immutable, and true,- who is Krishna, who is the creator and the ruler of this universe; who is seeking the welfare of his creation by means of his incomparable and indestructible power; whose actions are celebrated by all sages; who has bound human beings in a chain, of which one end is life and the other death; on whom the Rishis meditate, and a knowledge of whom imparts unalloyed happiness to their hearts, and for whose gratification and favor all the daily devotions are performed by all worshippers. If a man reads the Mahâbhârata and has faith in its doctrines, he is free from all sin, and ascends to heaven after his death.'"

The present volume contains such translation, as have from time to time made out of this prodigious epic, which is seven-fold greater in bulk than the Illiad and Odyssey taken together. All the stories here extracted are new to English literature, with the exception of a few passages of the Sâvitrî and the "Nala and Damayanti," which was long ago most faithfully rendered by Dean Milman, the version being published side by side with a clear and excellent Sanskrit text edited by Professor Monier Williams, C. I. E. But that presentation of the beautiful and brilliant legend - with all its conspicuous merits - seems better adapted to aid the student than adequately to reproduce the swift march of narrative, and old-world charm of the Indian tale, which I, also, have therefore ventured to transcribe; with all deference and gratitude to my predecessors.

I believe certain portions of the mighty poem which here appear, and many other episodes, to be of far greater antiquity than has been ascribed to the Mahâbhârata generally. Doubtless the "two hundred and twenty thousand lines" of the entire compilation contain in many places little and large additions and corrections, interpolated in Brahmanic or post- Buddhistic times; and he who ever so slightly explores this poetical ocean will, indeed, perceive defects, excrescences, differences, and breaks of artistic style or structure. But in the simpler and nobler sections the Sanskrit verse (ofttimes as musical and highly wrought as Homer's own Greek) bears, as I think, testimony-by evidence too long and recondite for citation here-to an origin anterior to writing, anterior to Purânic theology, anterior to Homer, perhaps even to Moses.

EDWIN ARNOLD.

LONDON, August, 1883.

SÂVITRÎ; OR, LOVE AND DEATH

"I mourn not for myself'," quoth Yudhisthir,
"Nor for my hero-brothers; but because
Draupadi hath been taken from us now.
Never was seen or known another such,
As queenly, true, and faithful to her vows,
As Draupadi."

Then said Markandya:
Wilt thou hear, Prince, of such another soul,
Wherein the nobleness of Draupadi
Dwell, of old days,- the Princess Sâvitrî?

THERE was a Raja, pious-minded, just,
King of the Mâdras,-valiant, wise, and true;
Victorious over sense, a worshipper;
Liberal in giving, prudent., dear alike
To peasant and to townsman; one whose joy
Lived in the weal of all men-Aswapati -
Patient, and free of any woe, he reigned,
Save that his manhood passing, left him]one,
A childless lord; for this he grieved; for this
Heavy observances he underwent,
Subduing needs of flesh, and oftentimes
Making high sacrifice to Sâvitrî;
While, for all food, at each sixth watch he took
A little measured dole; and thus he did
Through sixteen years, most excellent of Kings
Till at the last, divinest Sâvitrî
Grew well-content, and, taking shining shape,
Rose through the flames of sacrifice and showed
Unto that prince her heavenly countenance.
"Raja," the Goddess said - the Gift-bringer -
Thy piety, thy purity, thy fasts,
The largesse of thy hands, thy heart's wide love,

Thy strength of faith, have pleased me. Choose some boon.
Thy dearest wish, Monarch of Mâdra, ask;
It is not meet such merit go in vain."

The Raja answered: "Goddess, for the sake
Of children I did bear these heavy vows:
If thou art well-content, grant me, I pray,
Fair babes, continuers of my royal line;
This is the boon I choose, obeying law:
For - say the holy seers - the first great law
Is that a man leave seed."

The Goddess said:
I knew thine answer, Raja, ere it came;
And He, the Maker of all, hath heard my word
That this might be. The self-existent One
Consenteth. Born there shall be unto thee
A girl more sweet than any eyes have seen;
There is not found on earth so fair a maid
I that rejoice in the Great Father's will
Know this and tell thee."

"Oh, so may it be
The Raja cried, once and again; and she,
The Goddess, smiled anew, and vanished so.-
While Aswapati to his palace went.
'there dwelled he, doing justice to all folk;
Till, when the hour was good, the wise King lay
With her that was his first and fairest wife,
And she conceived a girl (a girl, my liege
Better than many boys), which wonder grew
In darkness, - as the Moon among the stars
Grows from a ring of silver to a round
In the month's waxing days, - and when time came
The Queen a daughter bore, with lotus-eyes,
Lovely of mould. joyous that Raja made
The birth-feast; and because the fair gift fell
From Sâvitrî the Goddess, and because
It was her day of sacrifice, they gave
The name of "Sâvitrî" unto the child.

In grace and beauty grew the maid, as if
Lakshmi's own self had taken woman's form.
And when swift years her gracious youth made ripe,
Like to an image of dark gold she seemed
Gleaming, with waist so fine, and breasts so deep,
And limbs so rounded. When she moved, all eyes
Gazed after her, as though an Apsara
Had lighted out of Swarga. Not one dared,
Of all the noblest lords, to ask for wife
That miracle, with eyes purple and soft
As lotus-petals, that pure perfect maid,
Whose face shed heavenly light where she did go.

Once she had fasted, laved her head, and bowed
Before the shrine of Agni, - as is meet,
And sacrificed, and spoken what is set
Unto the Brahmans - taking at their hands
The unconsumed offerings, and so passed
Into her father's presence - bright as 'Sri,
If 'Sri were woman! - Meekly at his feet
She laid the blossoms; meekly bent her head,
Folded her palms, and stood, radiant with grace,
Beside the Raja. He, beholding her
Come to her growth, and thus divinely fair,
Yet sued of none, was grieved at heart and spake
"Daughter, 'tis time we wed thee, but none comes
Asking thee; therefore, thou thyself some youth
Choose for thy lord, a virtuous prince: whoso
Is dear to thee, he shall be dear to me
For this the rule is- by the sages taught
Hear the commandment, noble maid - 'That sire
Who giveth not his child in marriage
Is blamable; and blamable that king
Who weddeth not; and blamable that son
Who, when his father dieth, guardeth not
His mother.' Heeding this," the Raja said,
Haste thee to choose, and so choose that I bear
No guilt, dear child, before the all-seeing Gods."

Thus spake he - from the royal presence then
Elders and ministers dismissing. She,
Sweet Sâvitrî, -low lying at his feet,
With soft shame heard her father, and obeyed.

Then, on a bright car mounting, companied
By ministers and sages, Sâvitrî
Journeyed through groves and pleasant woodland-towns
Where pious princes dwelled, in every spot
Paying meet homage at the Brahmans' feet;
And so from forest unto forest passed,
In all the Tirthas making offerings:
Thus did the Princess visit place by place.

THE King of Mâdra sat among his lords
With Narada beside him, counselling:
When - (son of Bhârat!) entered Sâvitrî
From passing through each haunt and hermitage,
Returning with those sages. At the sight
Of Narad seated by the Raja's side,
Humbly she touched the earth before their feet
With bended forehead.

Then spake Narada:
"Whence cometh thy fair child? and wherefore, King,
Being so ripe in beauty, giv'st thou not
The Princess to a husband?"

"Even for that
She journeyed," quoth the Raja; "being come,
Hear for thyself, great Rishi, what high lord
My daughter chooseth." Then, being bid to speak
Of Narad and the Raja, Sâvitrî
Softly said this: " In Chalva reigned a prince,
Lordly and just, Dyumutsena named,
Blind, and his only son not come to age;
And this sad king an enemy betrayed
Abusing his infirmity, whereby
Of throne and kingdom was that king bereft;
And with his queen and son, a banished man,

He fled into the wood; and, 'neath its shades,
A life of holiness cloth daily lead.
This Raja's son, born in the court, but bred
'Midst forest peace, - royal of blood, and named
Prince Satyavan, - to him my choice is given."

"Aho!" cried Narad, "evil is this choice
Which Sâvitrî hath made, who, knowing not,
Doth name the noble Satyavan her lord:
For, noble is the Prince, sprung of a pair
So just and faithful found in word and deed
The Brahmans styled him 'Truth-born ' at his birth.
Horses he loved, and ofttimes would he mould
Coursers of clay, or paint them on the wall;
Therefore 'Chitraswa' was he also called."

Then spake the King: "By this he shall have grown
Being of so fair birth - either a prince
Of valor, or a wise and patient saint."

Quoth Narad: "Like the sun is Satyavan
For grace and glory; like Vrihaspati
For counsel; like Mahendra's self for might;
And hath the patience of th' all-bearing earth."

"Is he a liberal giver? " asked the King;
Loveth he virtue? wears he noble airs?
Goeth he like a prince, with sweet proud looks?"

"He is as glad to give, if he hath store,
As Rantideva," Narada replied.
Pious he is; and true as Shivi was,
The son of Usinara; fair of form
(Yayâti was not fairer); sweet of looks
(The Aswins not more gracious); gallant, kind,
Reverent, self-governed, gentle, equitable,
Modest, and constant. justice lives in him,
And Honor guides. Those who do love a man
Praise him for manhood; they that seek a saint
Laud him for purity, and passions tamed."

"A prince thou showest us," the Raja said,
"All virtues owning. Tell me of some faults,
If fault he hath."

"None lives," quoth Narada.
But some fault mingles with his qualities
And Satyavan bears that he cannot mend.
The blot which spoils his brightness, the defect
Forbidding yonder Prince, Raja, is this,
'Tis fated he shall die after a year;
Count from to-day one year, he perisheth!"

"My Sâvitrî," the King cried; "go, dear child,
Some other husband choose. This hath one fault;
But huge it is, and mars all nobleness:
At the year's end he dies 'tis Narad's word,
Whom the gods teach."

But Sâvitrî replied:
Once falls a heritage; once a maid yields
Her maidenhood; once doth a father say,
Choose, I abide thy choice.' These three things done,
Are done forever. Be my Prince to live
A year, or many years; be he so great
As Narada hath said, or less than this;
Once have I chosen him, and choose not twice
My heart resolved, my mouth hath spoken it,
My hand shall execute; -this is my mind!"

Quoth Narad: "Yea, her mind is fixed, O King,
And none will turn her from the path of truth!
Also the virtues of Prince Satyavan
Shall in no other man be found. Give thou
Thy child to him. I gainsay not."

Therewith
The Raja sighed: "Nay, what must be, must be.
She speaketh sooth: and I will give my child,
For thou our Guru art."

Narada said:
Free be the gift of thy fair daughter, then;
May happiness yet light! -Raja, I go."
So went that sage, returning to his place
And the King bade the nuptials be prepared.

HE bade that all things be prepared, - the robes,
The golden cups; and summoned priest and sage,
Brahman and Rity-yaj and Purôhit;
And, on a day named fortunate, set forth
With Sâvitrî. In the mid-wood they found
Dyumutsena's sylvan court: the King,
Alighting, paced with slow steps to the spot
Where sat the blind lord underneath a sâl,
On mats woven of kusa grass. Then passed
Due salutations; worship, as is meet: -
All courteously the Raja spake his name,
All courteously the blind King gave to him
Earth, and a seat, and water in a jar;
Then asked, " What, Maharaja, bringeth thee?"
And Aswapati, answering, told him all.
With eyes fixed full upon Prince Satyavan
He spake: "This is my daughter, Sâvitrî
Take her from me to be wife to thy son,
According to the law; thou know'st the law.
Dyumutsena said: " Forced from our throne,
Wood-dwellers, hermits, keeping state no more,
We follow right, and how would right be done
If this most lovely lady we should house
Here, in our woods, unfitting home for her?
Answered the Raja: " Grief and joy we know,
And what is real and seeming, - she and I
Nor fits this fear with our unshaken minds.
Deny thou not the prayer of him who bows
In friendliness before thee; put not by
His wish who comes well-minded unto thee;
Thy stateless state shows noble; thou and I
Are of one rank; take then this maid of mine
To be thy daughter, since she chooseth me
Thy Satyavan for son."

The blind lord spake:
It was of old my wish to grow akin,
Raja, with thee, by marriage of our blood;
But ever have I answered to myself,
'Nay, for thy realm is lost , - forego this hope
Yet now, so let it be, since so thou wilt;
My welcome guest thou art. Thy will is mine."

Then gathered in the forest all those priests,
And with due rites the royal houses bound
By nuptial tie. And when the Raja saw
His daughter, as befits a princess, wed,
Home went he, glad. And glad was Satyavan,
Winning that beauteous spouse, with all gifts rich
And she rejoiced to be the wife of him,
So chosen of her soul. But when her sire
Departed, from her neck and arms she stripped
jewels and gold, and o'er her radiant form
Folded the robe of bark and yellow cloth
Which hermits use; and all hearts did she gain
By gentle actions, soft self-government,
Patience, and peace. The Queen had joy of her
For tender services and mindful cares;
The blind King took delight to know her days
So holy, and her wise words so restrained;
And with her lord in sweet converse she lived
Gracious and loving, dutiful and dear.

But while in the deep forest softly flowed
This quiet life of love and holiness,
The swift moons sped - and always in the heart
Of Sâvitrî, by day and night, there dwelt
The words of Narada, - those dreadful words!

Now, when the pleasant days were passed, which brought
The day of Doom, and Satyavan must die
(For hour by hour the Princess counted them,
Keeping the words of Narada in heart),
Bethinking on the fourth noon he should die,

She set herself to make the " Threefold Fast,"
Three days and nights foregoing food and sleep;
Which, when the King Dyumutsena heard,
Sorrowful he arose, and spake her thus:
"Daughter, a heavy task thou takest on
Hardly the saintliest soul might such abide."
But Sâvitrî gave answer: "Have no heed:
What I do set myself I will perform;
The vow is made, and I shall keep the vow."
"If it be made," quoth he, " it must be kept;
We cannot bid thee break thy word, once given."
With that the King forbade not, and she sat
Still, as though carved of wood, three days and nights.
But when the third night passed, and brought the day
Whereon her lord must die, she rose betimes,
Made offering on the altar flames, and sang
Softly the morning prayers; then, with clasped palms
Laid on her bosom, meekly came to greet
The King and Queen, and lowlily salute
"The gray-haired Brahmans. Thereupon those saints -
Resident in the woods - made answer mild
Unto the Princess: " Be it well with thee,
And with thy lord, for these good deeds of thine."
"May it be well! " she answered; in her heart
Full mournfully that hour of fate awaiting
Foretold of Narad.

Then they said to her:
Daughter, thy vow is kept. Come, now, and eat."
But Sâvitrî replied: " When the sun sinks
This evening, I will eat, - that is my vow."

So when they could not change her, afterward
Came Satyavan, the Prince, bound for the woods,
An axe upon his shoulder; unto whom
Wistfully spake the Princess: "Dearest Lord,
Go not alone to-day; let me come too
I cannot be apart from thee to-day."

"Why not 'to-day'?" quoth Satynvm. "The wood

Is strange to thee, Belovèd, and its paths
Rough for thy tender feet; besides, with fast
Thy soft limbs faint; how wilt thou walk with me?"

I am not weak nor weary," she replied,
And I can walk. Say me not nay, sweet Lord,
I have so great a heart to go with thee."

"If thou hast such good heart," answered the Prince,
I shall say yea; but first entreat the leave
Of those we reverence, lest a wrong be done."
So, pure and dutiful, she sought that place'
Where sat the King and Queen, and, bending low,
Murmured request: "My husband goeth straight
To the great forest, gathering fruits and flowers;
I pray your leave that I may be with him.
To make the Agnihôtra sacrifice
Fetcheth he those, and will not be gainsaid,
But surely goeth. Let me go. A year
Hath rolled since I did fare from th' hermitage
To see our groves in bloom. I have much will
To see them now."

The old King gently said:
In sooth it is a year since she was given
To be our son's wife, and I mind me not
Of any boon the loving heart hath asked,
Nor any one untimely word she spake;
Let it be as she prayeth. Go, my child;
Have care of Satyavan, and take thy way."

So, being permitted of them both, she went, -
That beauteous lady, - at her husband's side,
With aching heart, albeit her face was bright.
Flower-laden trees her large eyes lighted on,
Green glades where pea-fowl sported, crystal streams,
And soaring hills whose green sides burned with bloom,
Which oft the Prince would bid her gaze upon;
But she as oft turned those great eyes from them
To look on him, her husband, who must die,

14

(For always in her mind were Narad's words).
And so she walked behind him, guarding him,
Bethinking at what hour her lord must die,
Her true heart torn in twain, one half to him
Close-cleaving, one half watching if Death come.

THEN, having reached where woodland fruits did grow,
They gathered those, and filled a basket full;
And afterwards the Prince plied hard his axe,
Cutting the sacred fuel. Presently
There crept a pang upon him; a fierce throe
Burned through his brows, and, all a-sweat, he came
Feebly to Sâvitrî, and moaned: "O wife,
I am thus suddenly too weak for work;
My veins throb, Sâvitrî; my blood runs fire;
It is as if a threefold fork were plunged
Into my brain. Let me lie down, fair Love!
Indeed, I cannot stand upon my feet."

Thereon that noble lady, hastening near,
Stayed him, that would have fallen, with quick arms;
And, sitting on the earth, laid her lord's head
Tenderly in her lap. So bent she, mute,
Fanning his face, and thinking 'twas the day
The hour - which Narad named - the sure fixed date
Of dreadful end - when, lo! before her rose
A shade majestic. Red his garments were,
His body vast and dark; like fiery suns
The eyes which burned beneath his forehead-cloth
Armed was he with a noose, awful of mien.
This Form tremendous stood by Satyavan,
Fixing its gaze upon him. At the sight
The fearful Princess started to her feet.
Heedfully laying on the grass his head,
Up started she, with beating heart, and joined
Her palms for supplication, and spake thus
In accents tremulous: "Thou seem'st some god
Thy mien is more than mortal; make me know
What god thou art, and what thy purpose here."

And Yama said (the dreadful God of death)
Thou art a faithful wife, O Sâvitrî,
True to thy vows, pious, and dutiful;
Therefore I answer thee. Yama I am!
This Prince, thy lord, lieth at point to die
Him will I straightway bind and bear from life;
This is my office, and for this I come."
Then Sâvitrî spake sadly: "It is taught,
Thy messengers are sent to fetch the dying;
Why is it, Mightiest, thou art come thyself?

In pity of her love, the Pitiless
Answered, - the King of all the Dead replied:
"This was a Prince unparalleled, thy lord
Virtuous as fair, a sea of goodly gifts,
Not to be summoned by a meaner voice
Than Yama's own: therefore is Yama come."

With that the gloomy God fitted his noose,
And forced forth from the Prince the soul of him
Subtile, a thumb in length - which being reft,
Breath stayed, blood stopped, the body's grace was gone,
And all life's warmth to stony coldness turned.
Then, binding it, the Silent Presence bore
Satyavan's soul away toward the South.

But Sâvitrî the Princess followed him;
Being so bold in wifely purity,
So holy by her love: and so upheld,
She followed him.

Presently Yama turned.
"Go back," quoth he; "pay him the funeral dues.
Enough, O Sâvitrî! is wrought for love;
Go back! too far already hast thou come."

Then Sâvitrî made answer: " I must go
Where my lord goes, or where my lord is borne;
Nought other is my duty. Nay, I think,
By reason of my vows, my services

Done to the Gurus, and my faultless love,
Grant but thy grace, I shall unhindered go.
The sages teach that to walk seven steps,
One with another, maketh good men friends;
Beseech thee, let me say a verse to thee:-

Be master of thyself, if thou wilt be
Servant of Duty. Such as thou shalt see
Not self-subduing, do no deeds of good
In youth or age, in household or in wood.
But wise men know that virtue is best bliss,
And all by some one way may reach to this.
It needs not men should pass through orders four
To come to knowledge: doing right is more
Than any learning; therefore sages say
Best and most excellent is Virtue's way.

Spake Yama then: "Return! yet I am moved
By those soft words; justly their accents fell,
And sweet and reasonable was their sense.
See, now, thou faultless one. Except this life
I bear away, ask any boon from me;
It shall not be denied."

Sâvitrî said
Let, then, the King, my husband's father, have
His eyesight back, and be his strength restored,
And let him live anew, strong as the sun."

"I give this gift," Yama replied: "thy wish,
Blameless, shall be fulfilled. But now go back;
Already art thou wearied, and our road
Is hard and long. Turn back, lest thou, too, die."

The Princess answered: "Weary am I not,
So I walk nigh my lord. Where he is borne,
Thither wend I. Most mighty of the gods,
I follow whereso'er thou takest him.
A verse in writ on this, if thou wouldst hear: -

There is nought better than to be
With noble souls in company:
There is nought dearer than to wend
With good friends faithful to the end.
This is the love whose fruit is sweet;
Therefore to bide therein is meet."

Spake Yama, smiling: "Beautiful! thy words
Delight me; they are excellent, and teach
Wisdom unto the wise, singing soft truth.
Look, now! except the life of Satyavan,
Ask yet another - any - boon from me."

Sâvitrî said: "Let, then, the pious King,
My husband's father, who hath lost his throne,
Have back the Râj; and let him rule his realm
In happy righteousness. This boon I ask."

"He shall have back the throne," Yama replied,
And he shall reign in righteousness: these things
Will surely fall. But thou, gaining thy wish,
Return anon; so shalt thou 'scape sore ill."

"Ah, awful God! who hold'st the world in leash,"
The Princess said, "restraining evil men,
And leading good men, - even unconscious, - there
Where they attain, hear yet these famous words: -

The constant virtues of the good are tenderness and love
To all that lives - in earth, air, sea -great, small - below, above;
Compassionate of heart, they keep a gentle thought for each,
Kind in their actions, mild in will, and pitiful of speech
Who pitieth not he hath not faith; full many an one so
But when an enemy seeks help the good man gladly gives.

"As water to the thirsting," Yama said,
Princess, thy words melodious are to me.
Except the life of Satyavan thy lord,
Ask one boon yet again, for I will grant."

Answer made Sâvitrî: "The King, my sire,
Hath no male child. Let him see many sons
Begotten of his body, who may keep
The royal line long regnant. This I ask."

So it shall be the Lord of death replied;
A hundred fair preservers of his race
Thy sire shall boast. But this wish being won,
Return, dear Princess; thou hast come too far."

"It is not far for me," quoth Sâvitrî,
"Since I am near my husband; nay, my heart
Is set to go as far as to the end;
But hear these other verses, if thou wilt:-

By that sunlit name thou bearest,
Thou, Vaivaswata! art dearest;
Those that as their Lord proclaim thee,
King of Righteousness do name thee:
Better than themselves the wise
Trust the righteous. Each relies
Most upon the good, and makes
Friendship with them. Friendship takes
Fear from hearts; yet friends betray,
In good men we may trust alway."

Sweet lady," Yama said, "never were words
Spoke better; never truer heard by ear;
Lo! I am pleased with thee. Except this soul,
Ask one gift yet again, and get thee home."

"I ask thee, then," quickly the Princess cried,
Sons, many sons, born of my body: boys;
Satyavan's children; lovely, valiant, strong;
Continuers of their line. Grant this, kind God."

"I grant it," Yama answered; "thou shalt bear
Those sons; thy heart desireth, valiant, strong.
Therefore go back, that years be given thee.
Too long a path thou treadest, dark and rough."

But, sweeter than before, the Princess sang:-

In paths of peace and virtue
Always the good remain;
And sorrow shall not stay with them,
For long access of pain;
At meeting or at parting
Joys to their bosom strike;
For good to good is friendly,
And virtue loves her like.
The great sun goes his journey
By their strong truth impelled;
By their pure lives and penances
Is earth itself upheld;
Of all which live or shall live
Upon its hills and fields,
Pure hearts are the 'protectors,'
For virtue saves and shields.

"Never are noble spirits
Poor while their like survive;
True love has gems to render,
And virtue wealth to give.
Never is lost or wasted
The goodness of the good;
Never against a mercy,
Against a right, it stood;
And seeing this, that virtue
Is always friend to all,
The virtuous and true-hearted,
Men their 'protectors' call."

Line for line, Princess! as thou sangest so,"
Quoth Yarna, " all that lovely praise of good,
Grateful to hallowed minds, lofty in sound,
And couched in dulcet numbers - word by word
Dearer thou grew'st to me. O thou great heart,
Perfect and firm! ask any boon from me, -
Ask an incomparable boon!"

She cried
Swiftly, no longer stayed: "Not heaven I crave,
Nor heavenly joys, nor bliss incomparable,
Hard to be granted even by thee; but him,
My sweet lord's life, without which I am dead;
Give me that gift of gifts! I will not take
Aught less without him, - not one boon, - no praise,
No splendors, no rewards, - not even those sons
Whom thou didst promise. Ah, thou wilt not, now,
Bear hence the father of them, and my hope
Make thy free word good; give me Satyavan
Alive once more."

And thereupon the God
The Lord of justice, high Vaivaswata
Loosened the noose and freed the Prince's soul,
And gave it to the lady, saying this,
With eyes grown tender: "See, thou sweetest queen
Of women, brightest jewel of thy kind!
Here is thy husband. He shall live and reign
Side by side with thee, - saved by thee, - in peace,
And fame, and wealth, and health, many long years;
For pious sacrifices world-renowned.
Boys shalt thou bear to him, as I did grant, -
Kshatriya kings, fathers of kings to be,
Sustainers of thy line. Also, thy sire
Shall see his name upheld by sons of sons,
Like the immortals, valiant, Mâlavas."

These gifts the awful Yama gave, and went
Unto his place; but Sâvitrî -made glad,
Having her husband's soul - sped to the glade
Where his corse lay. She saw it there, and ran,
And, sitting on the earth, lifted its head,
And lulled it on her lap full tenderly.
Thereat warm life returned: the white lips moved;
The fixed eyes brightened, gazed, and gazed again;
As when one starts from sleep and sees a face -
The well-beloved's -grow clear, and, smiling, wakes,

So Satyavan. "Long have I slumbered, Dear,"
He sighed, "why didst thou not arouse me? Where
Is gone that gloomy man that haled at me?"
Answered the Princess: "Long, indeed, thy sleep,
Dear Lord, and deep; for he that haled at thee
Was Yama, God of Death: but he is gone;
And thou, being rested and awake, rise now,
If thou canst rise; for, look, the night is near!"

Thus, newly living, newly waked, the Prince
Glanced all around upon the blackening groves,
And whispered: "I came forth to pluck the fruits,
O slender-waisted, with thee: then, some pang
Shot through my temples while I hewed the wood,
And I lay down upon thy lap, dear wife,
And slept. This do I well remember. Next
Was it a dream, -that vast, dark, mighty One
Whom I beheld? Oh, if thou saw'st and know'st,
Was it in fancy, or in truth, he came?"

Softly she answered: "Night is falling fast;
To-morrow I will tell thee all, dear Lord.
Get to thy feet, and let us seek our home.
Guide us, ye Gods! the gloom spreads fast around
The creatures of the forest are abroad,
Which roam and cry by night. I hear the leaves
Rustle with beasts that creep. I hear this way
The yells of prowling jackals; beasts do haunt
In the southern wood; their noises make me fear."

"The wood is black with shadows," quoth the Prince
You would not know the path; you could not see it;
We cannot go."

She said: "There was to-day
A fire within this forest, and it burned
A withered tree; yonder the branches flame.
I'll fetch a lighted brand and kindle wood:
See! there is fuel here. Art thou so vexed
Because we cannot go? Grieve not. The path

Is hidden, and thy limbs are not yet knit.
To-morrow, when the way grows clear, depart;
But, if thou wilt, let us abide to-night."

And Satyavan replied: " The pains are gone
Which racked my brow; my limbs seem strong again;
Fain would I reach our home, if thou wilt aid.
Ever betimes I have been wont to come
At evening to the place where those we love
Await us. Ah, what trouble they will know,
Father and mother, searching now for us!
They prayed me hasten back. How they will weep,
Not seeing me; for there is none save me
To guard them. 'Quick return,' they said; 'our lives
Live upon thine; thou art our eyes, our breath,
Our hope of lineage; unto thee we look
For funeral cakes, for mourning feasts, for all.'
What will these do alone, not seeing me,
Who am their stay? Shame on the idle sleep
And foolish dreams which cost them all this pain
I cannot tarry here. My sire belike,
Having no eyes, asks at this very hour
News of me from each one that walks the wood.
Let us depart. Not, Sâvitrî, for us
Think I, but for those reverend ones at home,
Mourning me now. If they fare well, 'tis well
With me; if ill, nought's well; what would please them
Is wise and good to do."

Thereat he beat
Faint hands, eager to go; and Sâvitrî,
Seeing him weeping, wiped his tears away,
And gently spake: "If I have kept the fast,
Made sacrifices, given gifts, and wrought
Service to holy men, may this black night
Be bright to those and thee; for we will go.
I think I never spoke a false word once
In all my life, not even in jest; I pray
My truth may help to-night them, thee, and me!"

"Let us set forth," he cried - "if any harm
Hath fallen on those so dear, I could not live
I swear it by my soul! As thou art sweet,
Helpful, and virtuous, aid me to depart."

Then Sâvitrî arose, and tied her hair,
And lifted up her lord upon his feet;
Who, as he swept the dry leaves from his cloth,
Looked on the basket full of fruit. "But thou,"
The Princess said, "to-morrow shalt bring these
Give me thine axe, the axe is good to take."
So saying, she hung the basket on a branch,
And in her left hand carrying the axe,
Came back, and laid his arm across her neck,
Her right arm winding round him. So they went.

[The story concludes happily. Whilst the Prince and Princess find a path through the shades of the forest, the King, Dyumutsena, much afflicted at their absence, is suddenly restored to sight, and becomes consoled by his Rishis, who are convinced that Satyavan and Sâvitrî will return safe and well. Before dawn the absent pair do, indeed, come back; and, being eagerly questioned, the Prince is unable to explain what has befallen, but Sâvitrî relates it all, telling how Narada had foreseen that her husband must die, and how she had kept the "Threefold Fast," and gone with him to the wood, in order to avert his doom. Whilst the Rishis are praising the virtuous Princess, and loudly declaring that her piety and courage have conquered Death himself, messengers arrive from Dyumutsena's city, announcing, that the usurper has been overthrown there, and Satyavan's father re-proclaimed as King. Dyumutsena accordingly returns in triumph to his capital, with his Queen. with Sâvitrî, and with her husband, and all the good fortunes promised them by Yama duly arrive. Markandya finishes the narration by saying-]

So did fair Sâvitrî from Yama save
Her lord, and all his house to glory lead.
And Dratipadi - as wise and beautiful -
Shall, like that Princess, (O great Yudhisthir!)
Bring you past bitter seas to blessed shores.
Then was the Prince of Pandavas consoled.
He, also, who shall read with heart intent

Sâvitrî 's holy story, will wax glad,
And know that all fares well, and suffer nought.

NALA AND DAMAYANTI

A PRINCE there was, named Nala, Virasen's noble breed,
Goodly to see, and virtuous; a tamer of the steed
As Indra 'midst the gods, so he of kings was kingliest one,
Sovereign of men, and splendid as the golden, glittering sun;
Pure, knowing scripture, gallant; ruling nobly Nishadh's lands;
Dice-loving, but a proud, true chief of her embattled bands;
By lovely ladies lauded; free, trained in self-control;
A shield and bow; a Manu on earth; a royal soul!
And in Vidarbha's city the Raja Bhima dwelled;
Save offspring, from his perfect bliss no blessing was withheld;
For offspring, many a pious rite full patiently he wrought,
Till Damana the Brahman unto his house was brought.
Him Bhima, ever reverent, did courteously entreat,
Within the Queen's pavilion led him, to rest and eat
Whereby that sage, gown grateful, gave her - for joy of joys -
A girl, the gem of girlhood, and three brave, lusty boys,
Damana, Dama, Dânta, their names; - Damayanti she
No daughter more delightful, no sons could goodlier be.

Stately and bright and beautiful did Damayanti grow;
No land there was which did not the Slender-waisted know;
A hundred slaves her fair form decked with robe and ornament;
Like Sachi's self to serve her a hundred virgins bent
And 'midst them Bhima's daughter, in peerless glory dight,
Gleamed as the lightning glitters against the murk of night -
Having the eyes of Lakshmi, long-lidded, black, and bright:
Nay, -never Gods, nor Yakshas, nor mortal men among
Was one so rare and radiant e'er seen, or sued, or sung
As she, the heart-consuming, in heaven itself desired.

And Nala, too, of princes the Tiger-Prince, admired
Like Kama was; in beauty an embodied lord of love:
And ofttimes Nala praised they all other chiefs above
In Damayanti's hearing; and oftentimes to him

With worship and with wonder her beauty they would limn;
So that, unmet, unknowing, unseen, in each for each
A tender thought of longing grew up from seed of speech
And love (thou son of Kunti!) those gentle hearts did reach.

THUS Nala - hardly bearing in his heart
Such longing -wandered in his palace-woods,
And marked sonic water-birds, with painted plumes,
Disporting. One, by stealthy steps, he seized
But the sky-traveller spake to Nala this:
"Kill me not, Prince, and I will serve thee well.
For I, in Dainayanti's ear, will say
Such good of Nishadh's lord, that nevermore
Shall thought of man possess her, save of thee."

Thereat the Prince gladly gave liberty
To his soft prisoner, and all the swans
Flew, clanging, to Vidarbha, - a bright flock,
Straight to Vidarbha, where the Princess walked;
And there, beneath her eyes, those wingèd ones
Lighted. She saw them sail to earth, and marked
Sitting amid her maids - their graceful forms -
While those for wantonness 'gan chase the swans,
Which fluttered this and that way through the grove:
Each girl with tripping feet her bird pursued,
And Damayanti, laughing, followed hers;
Till-at the point to grasp-the flying prey
Deftly eluding touch, spake as men speak,
Addressing Bhima's daughter: -

"Lady dear!
Loveliest Damayanti! Nala dwells
In near Nishadha: oh, a noble Prince,
Not to be matched of men; an Aswin he,
For godliness. Incomparable maid
Wert thou but wife to that surpassing chief,
Rich would the fruit grow from such lordly birth,
Such peerless beauty. Slender-waisted one,
Gods, men, and Gandharvas have we beheld,
But never none among them like to him.

As thou art pearl of princesses, so he
Is crown of princes; happy would it fall,
One such perfection should another wed."

And when she heard that bird, (O King of men!)
The Princess answered: "Go, dear swan, and tell
This same to Nala;" . and the egg-born said,
I go and flew,- and told the Prince of all.

BUT Damayanti, having heard the bird,
Lived fancy-free no more; by Nala's side
Her soul dwelt, while she sat at home distraught,
Mournful and wan, sighing the hours away,
With eyes upcast, and passion-laden looks;
So that, eftsoons, her limbs failed, and her mind -
With -love o'erweighted - found no rest in sleep,
No grace in company, no joy at feasts.
Nor night nor day brought peace; always she heaved
Sigh upon sigh, till all her maidens knew -
By glance and mien and moan - how changed she was,
Her own sweet self no more. Then to the King
They told how Damayanti loved the Prince.
Which thing when Bhima from her maidens heard,
Deep pondering for his child what should be done,
And why the Princess was beside herself,
That lord of lands perceived his daughter grown,
And knew that for her high Swayamvara
The time was come.

So, to the Rajas all
The King sent word Ye Lords of Earth, attend
Of Damayanti the Swayamvara."
And when these learned of her Swayamvara,
Obeying Bhima, to his court they thronged,
Elephants, horses, cars, - over the land
In full files wending, bearing flags and wreaths
Of countless hues, with gallant companies
Of fighting men. And those high-hearted chiefs
The strong-armed King welcomed with worship fair,
As fitted each, and led them to their seats.

Now at that hour there passed towards Indra's heaven,
Thither from earth ascending, those twain saints,
The wise, the pure, the mighty-minded ones,
The self-restrained, - Narad and Parvata.
The mansion of the Sovereign of the Gods
In honor entered they,- and he, the Lord
Of Clouds, dread Indra, softly them salutes,
Inquiring of their weal, and of the world
Wherethrough their name was famous, how it fares.

Then Narad said: "Well is it, Lord of Gods,
With us, and with our world; and well with those
Who rule the peoples, O thou King in Heaven!
But He that slew the Demons spake again:
The princes of the earth, just-minded, brave,
Those who, in battle fearing not to fall,
See death on the descending blade, and charge
Full front against it, turning not their face, -
Theirs is this realm eternal, as to me
The cow of plenty, Kâmadhuk, belongs.
Where be my Kshatriya warriors? Wherefore now
See I none coming of those slaughtered lords,
Chiefs of mankind, our always honored guests?"

And unto Indra Narad gave reply:
King of the Air! no wars are waged below
None fall in fight, to enter here. The Lord
Of high Vidarbha hath a daughter, famed
For loveliness beyond all earthly maids,
The Princess Damayanti, far-renowned.
Of her, dread Sakra! the Swayamvara
Shall soon befall, and thither now repair
The kings and princes of all lands, to woo
Each for himself - this pearl of womanhood.
For oh, thou Slayer of the Demons, all
Desire the maid."

Drew round, while Narad spake,
The Masters, th' Immortals, pressing in

With Agni and the Greatest, near the throne,
To listen to the speech of Narada;
Whom having heard, all cried delightedly,
"We, too, will go." Thereupon those high gods,
With chariots, and with heavenly retinues,
Sped to Vidarbha, where the kings were met.
And Nala, knowing of this kingly tryst,
Went thither joyous, heart-full with the the might
Of Damayanti.

Thus it chanced the gods
Beheld the Prince wending along his road,
Goodly of mien, as is the Lord of Love.
The world's Protectors saw him, like a sun
For splendor; and, in very wonder, paused
Some time irresolute, so fair he was;
Then in mid-sky their golden chariots stayed,
And through the clouds descending called to him:
"Bho! Nala of Nishadha! Noblest Prince,
Be herald for us; bear our message now."

"YEA!" Nala made reply, "this will I do
And then - palm unto palm in reverence pressed
Asked: " Shining Ones, who are ye? Unto whom,
And what words bearing, will ye that I go?
Deign to instruct me what it is ye bid."
Thus the Prince spake, and Indra answered him:
"Thou seest th' immortal gods. Indra am I,
And this is Agni, and the other here,
Varuna, Lord of Waters; and beyond,
Yama, the King of Death, who parteth souls
From mortal frames. To Damayanti go;
Tell our approach. Say this: 'The world's dread lords,
Wishful to see thee, come; desiring thee, -
Indra, Varuna, Agni, Yama, all.
Choose of these powers to which thou wilt be given.'
But Nala, hearing that, joined palms again,
And cried: " Ah, send me not, with one accord
For this, most mighty Gods! How should a man
Sue for another, being suitor too?

How bear such errand? Have compassion, Gods!

Then spake they: "Yet thou saidst, 'This shall I do,'
Nishadha's Prince! and wilt thou do it not,
Forswearing faith? Nay, but depart, and soon!
So bid, but lingering yet again, he said:
Well guarded are the gates; how shall I find
Speech with her?"

"Thou shalt find," Indra replied.
And, lo! upon that word Nala was brought
To Damayanti's chamber. There he saw
Vidarbha's glory, sitting 'mid her maids,
In majesty and grace surpassing all;
So exquisite, so delicate of form,
Waist so fine-turned, such limbs, such lighted eyes,
The moon hath meaner radiance than she.
Love at the sight of that soft smiling face
Sprang to full passion, while he stood and gazed.
Yet, faith and duty urging, he restrained
His beating heart; but when those beauteous maids
Spied Nala, from their cushions they uprose,
Startled to see a man, yet startled more
Because he showed so heavenly bright and fair.
In wondering pleasure each saluted him,
Uttering no sound, but murmuring to themselves:
"Aho! the grace of him; aho! the brilliance
Aho! what glorious strength lives in his limbs
What is he? Is he God, Gandharva, Yaksha?"
But this unspoken, for they dared not breathe
One syllable, all standing shyly there
To see him, and to see his youth so sweet.
Yet, softly glancing back to his soft glance,
The Princess, presently, with fluttering breath,
Accosted Nala, saying: "Fairest Prince,
Who by thy faultless form hath filled my heart
With sudden joy, coming as come the gods,
Unstayed, I crave to know thee, who thou art;
How didst thou enter? how wert thou unseen?
Our palace is close-guarded, and the King

Hath issued mandates stem."

Tenderly spake
The Prince, replying to those tender words:
Most lovely! I am Nala. I am come
A herald of the gods unto thee here.
The gods desire thee, the immortal Four,
Indra, Varuna, Varna, Agni. Choose,
O Brightest! one from these to be thy lord.
By their help is it I have entered in
Unseen; none could behold me at thy gates,
Nor stay me, passing; and to speak their will
They sent me, fairest one and-best. Do thou,
Knowing the message, judge as seemeth well."

SHE bowed her head, hearing the great gods named,
And then, divinely smiling, said to him:
"Pledge thyself faithfully to me, and I
Will seek, O Raja, only how to pay
That debt with all I am, with all I have
For I and mine are thine, - in full trust thine.
Make me that promise, Prince. Thy gentle name -
Sung by the swan - first set my thoughts afire;
And for thy sake, - only for thee, - sweet Lord,
The kings were summoned hither. If, alas
Fair Prince, thou dost reject my sudden love,
So proffered, then must poison, flame, or flood,
Or knitted cord, be my sad remedy."

So spake Vidarbha's Pride - and Nala said:
"With gods so waiting, - with the world's dread lords
Hastening to woo, canst thou desire a man?
Bethink! I, unto these, that make and mar,
These all-wise ones, almighty, am like dust
Under their feet: lift thy heart to the height
Of what I bring. If mortal man offend
The most high gods, death is what springs of it.
Spare me to live, thou faultless lady! Choose
Which of these excellent great gods thou wilt
Wear the unstainèd robes! bear on thy brows

The wreaths which never fade, of heavenly blooms
Be, as thou mayst, a goddess, and enjoy
Godlike delights! Him who enfolds the earth,
Creating and consuming, Brightest Power,
Hutâsa, Eater of the Sacrifice,
What woman would not take? Or him whose rod
Herds all the generations forward still
On virtue's path, Red Yama, King of Death,
What woman would affront? Or him, the all-good,
All-wise destroyer of the Demons, first
In heaven, Mahendra, - who of womankind
Is there that would not wed? Or, if thy mind
Incline, doubt not to choose Varuna; he
Is of these world-protectors. From a heart
Full friendly cometh what I tell thee now."

Unto Nishadha's Prince the maid replied, -
Tears of distress dimming her lustrous eyes, -
"Humbly I reverence these mighty gods;
But thee I choose, and thee I take for lord;
And this I vow!"

With folded palms she stood,
And trembling lips, while his faint answer fell:
"Sent on such embassy, how shall I dare
Speak, sweetest Princess, for myself to thee?
Bound by my promise for the gods to sue,
How can I be a suitor for myself?
Silence is here my duty; afterwards,
If I shall come, in mine own name I'll come,
Mine own cause pleading. Ah, might that so be!"

Checking her tears, Damayanti sadly smiled,
And said full soft: "One way of hope I see,
A blameless way, O Lord of men! wherefrom
No fault shall rise, nor any danger fall.
Thou also, Prince, with Indra and these gods,
Must enter in where my Swayamvara
Is held; then I, in presence of those gods,
Will choose thee, dearest, for my lord; and so

Blame shall not light on thee."

With which sweet words
Soft in his ears, Nishadha straight returned
There where the gods were gathered, waiting him;
Whom the world's masters, on his way, perceived
And, spying, questioned, asking for his news:
Saw'st thou her, Prince? Didst see the sweet-lippcd one?
What spake she of us? Tell us true - tell all!"

Quoth Nala: "By your worshipful behest
Sent to her house, the great gates entered I,
Though the gray porters watched; but none might spy
My entering, by your power, O radiant Ones,
Saving the Raja's daughter; her I saw
Amid her maidens, and by them was seen.
On me with much amazement they did gaze
Whilst I your high Divinities extolled.
But she that hath the lovely face, with mind
Set upon me, hath chosen me, ye Gods.
For thus she spake, my Princess: 'Let them come,
And come thou, like a lordly tiger, too,
Unto the place of my Swayamvara;
There will I choose thee in their presence, Prince,
To be my lord - and so there will not fall
Blame, thou strong-armed! to thee.' This she did say
Even as I tell it; and what shall be next,
To will is yours, O ye immortal Ones!"

Soon, when the moon was good, and day and hour
Were found propitious, Bhima, King of men,
Summoned the chiefs to the Swayamvara;
Upon which message all those eager lords
For love of Damayanti hastened there.
Glorious with gilded pillars was the court,
Whereto a gate-house opened, and thereby
Into the square, like lions from the hills,
Paced the proud guests; and there their seats they took,
Each in his rank, the masters of the lands,
With crowns of fragrant blossoms garlanded,

And polished jewels swinging in their ears.
Of some the thews, knitted and rough, stood forth
Like iron maces; some had slender limbs,
Sleek and fine-turned like the five-headed snake;
Lords with long-flowing hair; glittering lords;
High-nosed, and eagle-eyed, and heavy-browed;
The faces of those kings shone in a ring
As shine at night the stars; and that great square
As thronged with Rajas was as Naga-land
Is full of serpents; thick with warlike chiefs
As mountain-caves with panthers. Unto these
Entered, in matchless majesty of form,
The Princess Damayanti. As she came,
The glory of her ravished eyes and hearts,
So that the gaze of all those haughty kings,
Fastening upon her loveliness, grew fixed, -
Not moving save with her, - step after step
Onward and always following the maid.

But while the styles and dignities of all
Were cried aloud, (O son of Bhârat!) lo!
The Princess marked five of that throng alike
in form and garb and visage. There they stood,
Each from the next undifferenced, but each
Nala's own self; - yet which might Nala be
In no wise could that doubting maid descry.
Who took her eye seemed Nala while she gazed,
Until she looked upon his like; and so
Pondered the lovely lady, sore-perplexed,
Thinking, "How shall I tell which be the gods,
And which is noble Nala?" Deep-distressed
And meditative waxed she, musing hard
What those signs were, delivered us of old,
Whereby gods may be known: "Of all those signs
Taught by our elders, lo! I see not one
Where stand yon five." So murmured she, and turned
Over and over every mark she knew.
At last, resolved to make the gods themselves
Her help at need, with reverent air and voice
Humbly saluted she those heavenly ones,

And with joined palms and trembling accents spake
As, when I heard the swans, I chose my Prince,
By that sincerity I call ye, Gods,
To show my Love to me and make me know!
As in my heart and soul and speech I stand
True to my choice, by that sincerity
I call the all-knowing gods to make me know
As the high gods created Nishadh's chief
To be my lord, by their sincerity
I bid them show themselves, and make me know!
As my vow, sealed to him, must be maintained
For his name, and for mine, I call the gods
By such sincerity to make me know
Let them appear, the masters of the world, -
The high gods, - each one in his proper shape,
That I may see Nishadha's chief, my choice,
Whom minstrels praise, and Damayanti loves."

Hearing that earnest speech, -so passion-fraught,
So full of truth, of strong resolve, of love,
Of singleness of soul and constancy, -
Even as she spake, the gods disclosed themselves.
By well-seen signs the effulgent Ones she knew.
Shadowless stood they, with unwinking eyes,
And skins which never moist with sweat; their feet
Light-gliding o'er the ground, not touching it;
The unfading blossoms on their brows not soiled
By earthly dust, but ever fair and fresh.
Whilst, by their side, garbed so and visaged so,
But doubled by his shadow, stained with dust,
The flower-cups wiltering in his wreath, his skin
Pearly with sweat, his feet upon the earth,
And eyes a-wink, stood Nala. One by one
Glanced she on those divinities, then bent
Her gaze upon the Prince, and, joyous, said:
I know thee, and I name my rightful lord,
Taking Nishadha's chief." Therewith she drew
Modestly nigh, and held him by the cloth,
With large eyes beaming love, and round his neck
Hung the bright chaplet, love's delicious crown;

So choosing him, - him only, - whom she named
Before the face of all to be her lord.
Oh, then brake forth from all those suitors proud,
"Ha!" and "Aho!" But from the gods and saints,
"Sadhu! well done! well done! " And all admired
The happy Prince, praising the grace of him
While Virasena's son, delightedly,
Spake to the slender-waisted these fond words
"Fair Princess! since, before all gods and men,
Thou makest me thy choice, right glad am I
Of this thy mind, and true lord will I be.
For so long, loveliest, as my breath endures,
Thine am I! Thus I plight my troth to thee."
So, with joined palms, unto that beauteous maid
His gentle faith he pledged, rejoicing her;
And, hand in hand, radiant with mutual love,
Before great Agni and the gods they passed,
The world's protectors worshipping.

Then those,
The lords of life, the powerful Ones, bestowed
Being well-pleased - on Nala, chosen so,
Eight noble boons. The boon which Indra gave
Was grace, at times of sacrifice, to see
The visible god approach, with step divine
And Agni's boon was this, that he would come
Whenever Nala called, - for everywhere
Hutâsa shineth, and all worlds are his;
Yama gave skill in cookery, steadfastness
In virtue; and Varuna, King of Floods,
Bade all the waters ripple at his call.
These boons the high gods doubled by the gift
Of bright wreaths wove with magic blooms of heaven:
And those bestowed, ascended to their seats.
Also with wonder and with joy returned
The Rajas and the Maharajas all,
Full of the marriage-feast; for Bhima made,
In pride and pleasure, stately nuptials;
So Damayanti and the Prince were wed.

Then, having tarried as is wont, that lord-
Nishadha's chief - took the King's leave, and went
Unto his city, bringing home with him
His jewel of all womanhood, with whom
Blissful he lived, as lives by Sachi's side
The slayer of the Demons. Like a sun
Shone Nala on his throne, ruling his folk
In strength and virtue, guardian of his state.
Also the Agwamedha Rite he made
Greatest of rites, the Offering of the Horse,
As did Yayâti; and all other acts
Of worship; and to sages gave rich gifts.

Many dear days of much delicious love,
In pleasant gardens and in shadowy groves,
Passed they together, sojourning like gods.
And Damayand bore unto her lord
A boy named Indrasen, and next, a girl
Named Indrasena. So in happiness
The good Prince governed, seeing all his land
Wealthy and well, in piety and peace.

Now at the choosing of Nishadha's chief
By Bhima's daughter, when those lords of life -
The effulgent gods - departed, Dwapara
They saw with Kali, coming. Indra said, -
The Demon-slayer, - spying these approach:
"Whither, with Dwapara, goest thou to-day,
O Kali? " And the sombre Shade replied:
"To Damayanti's high Swayamvara
I go, to make her mine, since she hath passed
Into my heart." But Indra, laughing, said:
"Ended is that Swayamvara; for she
Hath taken Raja Nala for her lord,
Before us all." But Kali, hearing this,
Brake into wrath -while he stood worshipping
That band divine - and furiously cried
"If she hath set a man above the gods,
To wed with him, for such sin let there fall
Doom, rightful, swift, and terrible, on her!"

"Nay," answered unto him those heavenly ones,
"But Damayanti chose with our good will;
And what maid but would choose so fair a prince,
Seeing he hath all qualities, and knows
Virtue, and rightly practises the vows,
And reads the four great Vedas, and, what's next,
The Holy Stories, whilst, perpetually,
The gods are honored in his house with gifts?
No hurt he does, kind to all living things
True of word is he, faithful, liberal, just
Steadfast and patient, temperate and pure
A king of men is Nala, like the gods.
He that would curse a prince of such a mould,
Thou foolish Kali, lays upon himself
A sin to crush himself; the curse comes back
And sinks him in the bottomless vast gulf
Of Narak."

Thus the gods to Kali spake,
And mounted heavenward; whereupon that Shade,
Frowning, to Dwapara burst forth: " My rage
Beareth no curb. Henceforth in Nala I
Will dwell; his kingdom I will make to fall;
His bliss with Damayanti I will mar;
And thou within the dice shalt enter straight,
And help me, Dwapara! to drag him down."

INTO which compact entering, those repaired -
Kali and Dwapara - to Nala's house,
And haunted in Nishadha, where he ruled,
Seeking occasion 'gainst the blameless Prince.
Long watched they; twelve years rolled ere Kali saw
The fateful fault arrive; Nishadha's Lord,
Easing himself, and sprinkling hands and lips
With purifying water, passed to prayer,
His feet unwashed, offending. Kali straight
Possessed the heedless Raja, entering him.

That hour there sat with Nala, Pushkara
His brother; and the evil spirit hissed

Into the ear of Pushkara "Ehi!
Arise, and challenge Nala at the dice.
Throw with the Prince! it may be thou shalt win
(Luck helping thee, and I) Nishadha's throne,
Town, treasures, palace, - thou mayst gain them all."
And Pushkara, hearing Kali's evil voice,
Made near to Nala, with the dice in hand
(A great piece for the "Bull," and little ones
For "Cows," and Kali hiding in the Bull).
So Pushkara came to Nala's side and said:
"Play with me, brother, at the ' Cows and Bull;'"
And, being put off, cried mockingly, "Nay, play!"
Shaming the Prince, whose spirit chafed to leave
A gage unfaced; but when Vidharbha's gem,
The Princess, heard that challenge, Nala rose:
"Yea, Pushkara, I will play fiercely he said;
And to the game addressed.

His gems he lost,
Armlets and belt and necklet; next the gold
Of the palace and its vessels; then the cars
Yoked with swift steeds and last, the royal robes
For, cast by cast, the dice against him fell,
bewitched by Kali; and, cast after cast,
The passion of the dice gat hold on him,
Until not one of all his faithfullest
Could stay the madman's hand and gamester's heart
Of who was named "Subduer of his Foes."

The townsmen gathered with the ministers
Into that palace gate they thronged (my King!)
To see their lord, if so they might abate
This sickness of his soul. The charioteer,
Forth standing from their midst, low worshipping,
Spake thus to Damayanti: "Great Princess,
Before thy door all the grieved city sits.
Say to our lord for us, 'Thy folk are here;
They mourn that evil fortunes hold their liege,
Who was so high and just.'" Then she, deject,
Passed in, and to Nishadha's ruler said,.

Her soft voice broken, and her bright eyes dimmed:
Raja, the people of thy town are here
Before our gates they gather, citizens
And counsellors, desiring speech With thee
In fealty they come. Wilt thou be pleased
We open to them? Wilt thou? " So she asked
Again and yet again; but not one word
To that sad lady with the lovely brows
Did Nala answer, wholly swallowed tip
Of Kali and the gaming; so that those -
The citizens and counsellors - cried out,
"Our lord is changed! He is not Nala now!"
And home returned, ashamed and sorrowful;
Whilst ceaselessly endured that foolish play
Moon after moon, -the Prince the loser still.

THEN Damayanti, seeing so estranged
Her lord, the praised in song, the chief of men,
Watching, all self-possessed, his fantasy,
And how the gaming held him; sad, and 'feared,
The heavy fortunes pondering of her Prince
Hating the fault, but to the offender kind
And fearing Nala should be stripped of all,
This thing devised. Vrihatsenâ she called,
Her foster-nurse and faithful ministrant, -
True, skilful at all service, soft of speech,
Kind-hearted - and she said, " Vrihatsenâ,
Go call the ministers to council now,
As though 'twere Nala bade; and make them count
What store is gone of treasure, what abides."
So went Vrihatsenâ, and summoned those;
And when they knew all things, as from the Prince,
"Truly we, too, shall perish!" cried they then;
And all to Nala went, and all the town,
A second time assembling, thronged his gates
Which Bhima's daughter told; but not one word
Answered the Prince. And when she saw her lord
Put by her plea, utterly slighting it,
Back to her chamber, full of shame, she goes,
And there still hears the dice are falling ill;

Still hears of Nala daily losing more;
So that again unto her nurse she spake:
"Send to Varshneya, good Vrihatsenâ;
Say to the charioteer, - in Nala's name, -
'A great thing is to do. Come thou!'" And this, -
So soon as Damayanti uttered it, -
Vrihatsenâ, by faithful servants, told
Unto the son of Vrishni, who, being come
In fitting time and place, heard the sweet Queen
In mournful music speak these wistful words:
"Thou knowest how thy Raja trusted thee;
Now he hath fall'n on evil; succor him!
The more that Pushkara conquers in the play,
The wilder rage of gaming takes thy lord:
The more for Pushkara the dice light well,
More contrary they happen to the Prince
Nor heeds he, as were meet, kindred or friends
Nay, of myself he putteth by the prayer
Unanswered, being bewitched; for well I deem
This is not noble-minded Nala's sin,
But some ill spell possesseth him to shut
His ears to me. Thou, therefore, charioteer!
Our refuge be; do what I shall command -
My heart is dark with fear. Yea, it may fall
Our lord will perish. Wherefore, harnessing
His chosen steeds, which fly as swift as thought,
Take these our children in the chariot
And drive to Kundina, delivering there
Unto my kin the little ones, and car,
And horses. Afterwards abide thou there,
Or otherwhere depart."

Varshneya heard
The words of Damayanti, and forthwith
In Nala's council-hall recounted them,
The chief men being present; who, thus met,
And long debating, gave him leave to go.
So with that royal pair to Bhima's town
Drove he, and at Vidarbha rendered up,
Together with the swift steeds and the car,

That sweet maid Indrasena, and the Prince
Indrasen, and made reverence to the King,
Saddened for sake of Nala. Afterward
Taking his leave, unto Ayodhyâ
Varshneya went, exceeding sorrowful,
And with King Rituparna (O my Prince!)
Took service as a charioteer.

THESE gone, -
The praised-of-poets, Nala, still played on,
Till Pushkara his kingdom's wealth had won,
And whatso was to lose beside. Thereat
With scornful laugh mocked he that beggared Prince,
Saying: "One other throw! once more! - Yet sooth,
What canst thou stake?' Nothing is left for thee
Save Damayanti; all the rest is mine.
Play we for Damayanti, if thou wilt."
But hearing this from Pushkara, the Prince
So in his heart by grief and shame was tom,
No word he uttered, - only glared in wrath
Upon his mocker, upon Pushkara.
Then, his rich robes and jewels stripping off,
Uncovered, with one cloth, 'mid waiting friends
Sorrowful passed he forth, his great state gone;
The Princess, with one garment, following him,
Piteous to see. And there without the gates
Three nights they lay, - Nishadha's King and Queen.
Upon the fourth day Pushkara proclaimed,
Throughout the city, "Whoso yieldeth help
To Nala, dieth! Let my will be known!"

So, for this bitter word of Pushkara's power
(O Yudhisthir!) the townsmen rendered not
Service nor love, but left them outcast there,
Unhelped, whom all the city should have helped.
Yet three nights longer tarried he, his drink
The common pool, his meat such fruits and roots
As miserable hunger plucks from earth:
Then fled they from those walls, the Prince going first,
The Princess following.

After grievous days,
Pinched ever with sharp famine, Nala saw
A flock of gold-winged birds lighting anigh,
And to himself the famished Raja said:
"Lo! here is food .- this day we shall have store
Then lightly cast his cloth and covered them.
But these, fluttering aloft, bore with them there
Nala's one cloth; and, hovering overhead,
Uttered sharp - stinging words, reviling him
Even as he stood, naked to all the airs,
Downcast and desperate: " Thou brain-sick Prince
We are the dice; we come to ravish hence
Thy last poor cloth; we were not well content
Thou shouldst depart owning a garment still."
And when he saw the dice take wings and fly,
Leaving him bare, to Damayanti spake
This melancholy Prince: " O Blameless One,
They by whose malice I am driven forth,
Finding no sustenance, sad, famine-gaunt,
They whose decree forbade Nishadha's folk
Should succor me, their Raja, -these have come, -
Demon and dice, - and like to wingèd birds
Have borne away my cloth. To such shame fall'n,
Such utmost woe, wretched, demented - I
Thy lord am still, and counsel thee for good.
Attend! Hence be there many roads which go
Southwards: some pass Avanti's walls, and some
Skirt Rikshavan, the forest of the bears;
This wends to Vindhya's lofty peaks; and this
To the green banks where quick Payoshni runs
Seaward, between her hermitages, rich
In fruits and roots; and yon path leadeth thee
Unto Vidarbha; that to Kosala,
And therefrom southward - southward - far away."

So spake he to the Princess wistfully,
Between his words pointing along the paths,
Which she should take (O King!). But Bhima's child
Made answer, bowed with grief, heir soft voice choked

With sobs, these piteous accents uttering
"My heart beats quick - my body's force is gone,
Thinking, dear Prince, on this which thou hast said,
Pointing along the paths. What I robbed of realm,
Stripped of thy wealth, bare, famished, parched with thirst.
Thus shall I leave thee in the untrodden wood?'
Ah, no! While thou dost muse on dear days fled,
Hungry and weeping, I in this wild waste
Will charm thy griefs away, solacing thee.
The wisest doctors say, 'In every woe
No better physic is than wifely love.'
And, Nala, I will make it true to thee."
"Thou mak'st it true," he said; "thou sayest well,
Sweet Damayanti; neither is there friend
To sad men given better than a wife.
I had no thought to leave thee, foolish Love
Why didst thou fear? Alas, 'tis from myself
That I would fly -not thee, thou Faultless One!"

"Yet, if," the Princess answered, "Maharaj!
Thou hadst no thought to leave me, why by thee
Was the way pointed to Vidarbha's walls?
I know thou wouldst not quit me, noblest Lord,
Being thyself, but only if thy mind
Were sure distraught; and see, thou gazest still
Along the southward road, my dread thereby
Increasing, thou that wert as are the gods!
If it be thy fixed thought, ' 'Twere best she went
Unto her people,' - be it so; I go;
Put hand in hand with thee. Thus let us fare
Unto Vidarbha, where the King, my sire,
Will greet thee well, and honor thee; and we
Happy and safe within his gates shall dwell."

"As is thy father's kingdom," Nala said,
So, once, was mine. Be sure, whate'er betide,
Never will I go thither! How, in sooth,
Should I, who came there glorious, gladdening thee,
Creep back, thy shame and scorn, disconsolate?"

So to sweet Damayanti spake the Prince,
Beguiling her, whom now one cloth scarce clad, -
For but one garb they shared; and thus they strayed
Hither and thither, faint for meat and drink,
Until a little hut they spied; and there,
Nishadha's monarch, entering, sat him down
On the bare ground, the Princess by his side, -
Vidarbha's glory, wearing that scant cloth,
Without a mat, soiled by the dust and mire.
At Damayanti's side he sank asleep,
Outworn; and beauteous Damayanti slept,
Spent with strange trials, - she so gently reared,
So soft and holy. But while slumbering thus,
No peaceful rest knew Nala. Trouble-tossed
He woke, forever thinking of his realm
Lost, lieges estranged, and all the griefs
Of that wild wood. These on his heart came back,
And, "What if I shall do it? What, again,
If I shall do it not? " So murmured he.
"Would death be better, or to leave my Love?
For my sake she endures this woe, my fate
Too fondly sharing; freed from me, her steps
Would turn unto her people. At my side,
Sure suffering is her portion; but apart,
It might be she would somewhere comfort find."

Thus with himself debating o'er and o'er,
The Prince resolves abandonment were best.
"For how," saith he, " should any in the wood
Harm her, so radiant in her grace, so good,
So noble, virtuous, faithful, famous, pure?
Thus mused his miserable mind, seduced
By Kali's cursèd mischiefs to betray
His sleeping wife. Then, seeing his loin-cloth gone,
And Damayanti clad, he drew anigh,
Thinking to take of hers, and muttering,
"May I not rend one fold, and she not know?
So meditating, round the cabin crept
Prince Nala, feeling up and down its walls;
And, presently, within the purlieus found

A naked knife, keen-tempered; therewithal
Shred he away a piece, and bound it on;
Then made with desperate steps to seek the waste,
Leaving the Princess sleeping; but, anon,
Turns back again in changeful mood and glides
Into the hut, and, gazing wistfully
On slumbering Damayanti, moans with tears:
"Ah, Sweetheart! whom nor wind nor sun before
Hath ever rudely touched; thou to be couched
In this poor hut, its floor thy bed, and I,
Thy lord, deserting thee, stealing from thee
Thy last robe! O my Love with the bright smile,
My slender-waisted Queen! Will she not wake
To madness? Yea, and when she wanders lone
In the dark wood, haunted with beasts and snakes,
How will it fare with Bhima's tender child,
The bright and peerless? O my life,my wife!
May the great sun, may the Eight Powers of air,
The Rudras, Maruts, and the Aswins twain,
Guard thee, thou true and dear one, on thy way!"

So to his sleeping Queen -on all the earth
Unmatched for beauty - spake he piteously;
Then brake away once more, by Kali driven.
But yet another and another time
Stole back into the hut, for one last gaze,
That way by Kali dragged, this way by love.
Two hearts he had, - the trouble- stricken Prince,
One beating " Go," one throbbing " Stay;" and thus
Backwards and forwards swung his mind between,
Till, mastered by the sorrow and the spell,
Frantic flies Nala, leaving there alone
That tender sleeper, sighing as she slept.
He flies -the soulless prey of Kali flies;
Still, while he hurries through the forest drear,
Thinking upon that sweet face he hath left.

FAR distant (King!) was Nala, when, refreshed,
The slender-waisted wakened, shuddering
At the wood's silence; but when, seeking him,

She found no Nala, sudden anguish seized
Her frightened heart, and, lifting high her voice,
Loud cried she: " Maharaja! Nishadh's Prince
Ha, Lord! ha, Maharaj! ha, Master! why
Hast thou abandoned me? Now am I lost,
Am doomed, undone, left in this lonesome gloom.
Wert thou not named, O Nala, true and just?
Yet art thou such, to quit me while I slept?
And hast thou so forsaken me, thy wife, -
Thine own fond wife, - who never wrought thee wrong
When by all others wrong was wrought on thee?
Mak'st thou it good to me, now, Lord of men,
That love which long ago before the gods
Thou didst proclaim? Alas! Death will not come,
Except at his appointed time to men,
And therefore for a little I shall live,
Whom thou hast lived to leave. Nay, 'tis a jest
Ah, Truant, Runaway, enough thou play'st
Come forth, my Lord! - I am afraid! Come forth!
Linger not, for I see - I spy thee there;
Thou art within yon thicket! Why not speak
One word, Nishadha? Nala, cruel Prince!
Thou know'st me lone, and comest not to calm
My terrors, and be with me in my need.
Aft gone indeed? Then I'll not mourn myself,
For whatso may befall me; I must think
How desolate thou art, and weep for thee.
What wilt thou do, thirsty and hungry, spent
With wandering, when, at nightfall, 'mid th, trees
Thou hast me not, sweet Prince, to comfort thee?"

Thereat, distracted by her bitter fears,
Like one whose heart is fire, forward and back
She runs, hither and thither, weeping, wild.
One while she sinks to earth, one while she springs
Quick to her feet; now utterly o'ercome
By fear and fasting, now by grief driven mad,
Wailing and sobbing; till anon, with moans
And broken sighs and tears, Bhima's fair child,
The ever-faithful wife, speaks thus again:

"By whomsoever's spell this harm hath fall'n
On Nishadh's Lord, I pray that evil one
May bear a bitterer plague than Nala doth!
To him, whoever set my guileless Prince
On these ill deeds, I pray some direr might
May bring far darker days, and life to live
More miserable still!"

Thus, woe-begone,
Mourned that great-hearted wife her vanished lord,
Seeking him ever in the gloomy shades,
By wild beasts haunted. Roaming everywhere,
Like one possessed, frantic, disconsolate,
Went Bhima's daughter. "Ha, ha! Maharaj!"
So crying runs she, so in every place
Is heard her ceaseless wail, as when is heard
The fish-hawk's cry, which screams, and circling screams,
And will not stint complaining.

Suddenly,
Straying too near his den, a serpent's coils
Seized Bhima's daughter. A prodigious snake,
Glittering and strong, and furious for food,
Knitted about the Princess. She, o'erwhelmed
With horror, and the cold enfolding death,
Spends her last breaths in pitiful laments
For Nala, not herself. "Ah, Prince!" she cried,
"That would have saved me, who must perish now,
Seized in the lone wood by this hideous snake,
Why art thou not beside me? What will be
Thy thought, Nishadha! me remembering
In days to come, when, from the curse set free,
Thou hast thy noble mind again, thyself,
Thy wealth, - all save thy wife? Then thou'lt be sad,
Be weary, wilt need food and drink; but I
Shall minister no longer. Who will tend
My Love, my Lord, my Lion among kings,
My blameless Nala, - Damayanti dead?"

That hour a hunter, roving through the brake,

Heard her bewailing, and with quickened steps
Made nigh, and, spying a woman, almond-eyed,
Lovely, forlorn, by that fell monster knit,
He ran; and, as he came, with keen shaft clove,
Through gaping mouth and crown, th' unwitting worm,
Slaying it. Then the woodman from its folds
Freed her, and laved the snake's slime from her limbs
With water of the pool, comforting her
And giving food; and afterwards (my King!)
Inquiry made: "What doest, in this wood,
Thou with the fawn's eyes? And how camest thou,
My mistress, to such pit of misery?"

And Damayanti, spoken fair by him,
Recounted all which had befallen her.

But, gazing on her graces, scantly clad
With half a cloth, those smooth, full sides, those breasts
Beauteously swelling, form of faultless mould,
Sweet youthful face, fair as the moon at full,
And dark orbs, by long curving lashes swept;
Hearing her tender sighs and honeyed speech,
The hunter fell to hot desire; he dared
Essay to woo, with whispered words at first,
And next by amorous approach, the Queen;
Who, presently perceiving what he would,
And all that baseness of him, - being so pure,
So chaste, and faithful, - like a blazing torch
Took fire of scorn and anger 'gainst the man,
Her true soul burning at him, till the wretch,
Wicked in heart, but impotent of will,
Glared on her, splendidly invincible
In weakness, loftily defying wrong,
A living flame of lighted chastity.
She then - albeit so desolate, so lone,
Abandoned by her lord, stripped of her state, -
Like a proud princess stormed, flinging away
All terms of supplication, cursing him
With wrath which scorched: "If I am clean in heart
And true in thought unto Nishadha's King,

Then mayst thou, vile pursuer of the beasts,
Sink to the earth, stone dead!"

While she did speak,
The hunter breathless fell to earth, stone dead,
As falls a tree-trunk blasted by the bolt.

THAT ravisher destroyed, the lotus-eyed
Fared forward, threading still the fearful wood,
-Lonely and dim, with trill of jhillikas[1]
Resounding, and fierce noise of many beasts
Laired in its shade, lions and leopards, deer,
Close-hiding tigers, sullen bisons, wolves,
And shaggy bears. Also the glades of it
Were filled with fowl which crept, or flew, and cried.
A home for savage men and murderers,
Thick with a world of trees, whereof was sal,[2]
Sharp-seeded, weeping gum; knotted bambus,

Dhavas with twisted roots; smooth aswatthas,
Large-leaved, and creeping through the cloven rocks;
Tindukas, iron-fibred, dark of grain;
Ingudas, yielding oil; and kinsukas,
With scarlet flowerets flaming. Thronging these
Were arjuns and arishta-clumps, which bear
The scented purple clusters; syandans,
And tall silk-cotton trees, and mango-belts
With silvery spears; and wild rose-apple, blent
Mid lodhra-tufts and khadirs, interknit
By clinging rattans, climbing everywhere
From stem to stem. Therewith were intermixed
Round pools where rocked the lotus - âmalaks,
Plakshas with fluted leaves, kadambas sweet,
Udumbaras and, on the jungle-edge,
Tangles of reed and jujube, whence there rose

---

[1] Jhillikas are the large wood-crickets.
[2] I have somewhat expanded this passage, which in the original Sanskrit is a bare enumeration of the different trees, in long compound words, each word filling a whole line.

Bel-trees and nyagrodhas, dropping roots
Down from the air; broad-leaved priyâlas, palms
And date-trees, and the gold myrobalan,
With copper-leaved vibhîtikas. All these
Crowded the wood; and many a crag it held,
With precious ore of metals interveined;
And many a creeper-covered cave wherein
The spoken word rolled round - and many a cleft
Where the thick stems were like a wall to see;
And many a winding stream and reedy jheel,
And glassy lakelet, where the woodland beasts
In free peace gathered.

Wandering onward thus,
The Princess saw far-gliding forms of dread,
Pisachas, Rakshasas, ill sprites and fiends
Which haunt, with swinging snakes, the undergrowth,
Dark pools she saw, and drinking-holes, and peaks
Wherefrom brake down in tumbling cataracts
The wild white waters, marvellous to hear.
Also she passed - this daughter of a king -
Where snorted the fierce buffaloes, and where
The gray boars rooted for their food, and where
The black bears growled, and serpents in the grass
Rustled and hissed. But all along that way
Safe paced she in her majesty of grace,
High fortune, courage, constancy, and right, -
Vidarbha's glory, - seeking, all alone,
Lost Nala and less terror at these sights
Came to sad Damayanti for herself
Threading this dreadful forest - than for him.
Most was her mind on Nala's fate intent.
Bitterly grieving stood the sweet Princess
Upon a rock, her tender limbs a-thrill
With heavy fears for Nala while she spake:-

"Broad-chested Chief! my long-armed Lord of men!
Nishadha's King! Ah! whither art thou gone,
Leaving me thus in the unpeopled wood?
The Aswamedha sacrifice thou mad'st,

And all the rites and royal gifts hast given,
A lion-hearted Prince, holy and true
To all save me! That which thou didst declare,
Hand in hand with me, - once so fond and kind, -
Recall it now, - thy sacred word, thy vow,
Whithersoever, Raja, thou art fled.
Think how the message of the gold-winged swans
Was spoken, by thine own lips, then to me!
True men keep faith; this is the teaching taught
In Vedas, Angas, and Upangas all,
Hear which we may; will thou not, therefore, Prince,
Wilt thou not, terror of thy foes, keep faith,
Making thy promise good to cleave to me?
Ha, Nala, Lord! Am I not surely still
Thy chosen, thy belovèd? Answerest not
Thy wife in this dark, horror-haunted shade?
The tyrant of the jungle, fierce and fell,
With jaws agape to take me, crouches nigh,
And thou not here to rescue me, -not thou,
Who saidst none other in the world was dear
But Damayanti! Prove the fond speech true,
Uttered so often! Why repliest not
To me, thy well-belovèd; me, distraught,
Longed for and longing; me, my Prince and pride,
That am so weary, weak, and miserable,
Stained with the mire, in this torn cloth half clad,
Alone and weeping, seeing no help near?
Ah, stag of all the herd I leav'st thou thy hind
Astray, regarding not these tears which roll?
My Nala, Maharaja! It is I
Who cry, thy Damayanti, true and pure,
Lost in the wood, and still thou answerest not
High-born, high-hearted, full of grace and strength
In all thy limbs, shall I not find thee soon
On yonder hill? Shall I not see, at last,
In some track of this grim, beast-peopled wood,
Standing, or seated, or upon the leaves
Lying, or coming, him who is of men
The glory, but for me the grief-maker?
If not, whom shall I question, woe-begone,

Saying, 'In any region of this wood
Hast thou, perchance, seen Nala?' Is there none,
In all the forest, would reply to me
With tidings of my lord, wandered away,
Kingly in mind and form, of hosts of foes
The conqueror? Who will say, with blessed voice,
'That Raja with the lotus-eyes is near,
Whom thou dost seek'? - Nay, here comes one to ask,
The yellow forest-king, his great jaws armed
With fourfold fangs. A tiger standeth now
Face to face on my path; I'll speak with him
Fearlessly: 'Dreadful chief of all this waste,
Thou art the sovereign of the beasts, and I
Am daughter of Vidarbha's King; my name,
The Princess Damayanti - know thou me,
Wife of Nishadha's Lord, -of Nala, -styled
"Subduer of his Foes"? Him seek I here, -
Abandoned, sorrow- stricken, miserable.
Comfort me, mighty beast, if so thou canst,
Saying thou hast seen Nala; but if this
Thou canst not do, then, ah, thou savage lord,
Terrible friend, devour me, setting me
Free from all woes!' The tiger answereth not;
He turns, and quits me in my tears, to stalk
Down where the river glitters through the reeds,
Seeking its seaward way. Then will I pray
Unto yon sacred mount of clustered crags,
Broad-shouldered, shining, lifting high to heaven
Its diverse-colored peaks, where the mind climbs,
Its hid heart rich with silver veins, and gold,
And stored with many a precious gem unseen.
Clear towers it o'er the forest, broad and bright
Like a green banner; and the sides of it
House many a living thing, - lions and boars,
Tigers and elephants, and bears and deer.
Softly around me from its feathered flocks
The songs ring, perched upon the kinsuk trees,
The asokas, vakuls, and punnâga boughs,
Or hidden in the karnikara, leaves,
And tendrils of the dhava or the fig;

Full of great glens it soars, where waters leap
And bright birds lave. This king of hills I sue
For tidings of my lord. O Mountain Lord,
Far-seen and celebrated hill I that cleav'st
The blue of the sky, refuge of living things,
Most noble eminence, I worship thee
Thee I salute, who am a monarch's child,
The daughter and the consort of a prince,
The high-born Damayanti, unto whom
Bhima, Vidarbha's chief, - that puissant lord,
Was sire, renowned o'er earth. Protector he
Of the four castes, performer of the rites
Called Rajasuya and the Aswamedh, -
A bounteous giver, first of rulers, known
For his large shining eyes - holy and just,
Fast to his word, unenvious, sweet of speech,
Gentle and valiant, dutiful and pure;
The guardian of Vidarbha, of his foes
The slayer. Know me, O Majestic Mount!
For that King's daughter, bending low to thee.
In Nishadh lived the father of my lord,
The Maharaja Virasena named,
Wealthy and great; whose son, of regal blood,
High-fortuned, powerful, and noble-souled,
Ruleth by right the realm paternal: he
Is Nala, terror of all enemies;
Dark Nala, praised-in-song; Nala the just,
The pure; deep-seen in scriptures, sweet of speech,
Drinker of Soma-juice, and worshipper
Of Agni; sacrificin giving gifts;
First in the wars, a perfect, princely lord.
His wife am I, Great Mountain! and come here
Fortuneless, husbandless, and spiritless,
Everywhere seeking him, my best of men.
O Mount, whose doubled ridge stamps on the sky,
Yon line, by fivescore splendid pinnacles
Indented! tell me, in this gloomy wood
Hast thou seen Nala? Nala, wise and bold,
Like a tusked elephant for might; long-armed,
Indomitable, gallant, glorious, true

Nala, Nishadha's chief, - hast thou seen him?
O Mountain, why consolest thou me not,
Answering one word to sorrowful, distressed,
Lonely, lost Damayanti?"

Then she cried:
But answer for thyself, Hero and Lord!
If thou be'st in the forest, show thyself!
Alas! when shall I hear that voice, as low,
As tender as the murmur of the rain
When great clouds gather; sweet as Amrit-drink?
Thy voice, once more, my Nala, calling to me
Full softly, 'Damayanti!'-dearest Prince,
That would be music soothing to these ears
As sound of sacred Veda; that would stay
My pains and comfort me, and bring me peace."

Thereafter, turning from the mount, she went
Northwards, and journeying on three nights and days
Came to a green incomparable grove
By holy men inhabited; a haunt
Placid as Paradise, whose indwellers
Like to Vasistha, Bhrigu, Atri, were, -
Those ancient saints. Restraining sense they lived,
Heedful in meats, subduing passion, pure,
Breathing within; their food water and herbs;
Ascetics; very holy; seeking still
The heavenward road; clad in the bark of trees
And skins, - all gauds of earth being put by.
This hermitage, peopled by gentle ones,
Glad Damayanti spied, circled with herds
Of wild things grazing fearless, and with troops
Of monkey-folk o'erhead; and when she saw,
Her heart was lightened, for its quietness.
So drew she nigh, - that lovely wanderer,
Bright-browed, long-tressed, large-hipped, full-bosomed fair,
With pearly teeth and honeyed mouth, in gait
Right queenly still, having those long black eyes, -
The wife of Virasena's son, the gem
Of all dear women, glory of her time;

Sad Damayanti entered their abode,
Those holy men saluting reverently,
With modest body bowed. Thus stood she there,
And all the saints spake gently, "Swâgatam, -
Welcome and gave the greetings which are meet;
And afterwards, "Repose thyself," they said -
"What wouldst thou have of us?" Then, with soft words
The slender-waisted spake: "Of all these here,
So worshipful in sacrifice and rite, -
'Mid gentle beasts and birds, - in tasks and toils
And blameless duties -is it well?" And they
Answered: "We thank you, noble lady, well.
Tell us, most beauteous one, thy name, and say
What thou desirest. Seeing thee so fair,
So worthy, yet so sorrowful, our minds
Are lost in wonder. Weep not. Comfort take.
Art thou the goddess of the wood? Art thou
The Mountain-Vakshi, or, belike, some sprite
Which lives under the river? Tell us true,
Gentle and faultless form!"

Whereat reply
Thus made she to the Rishis: "None of these
Am I, good saints. No goddess of the wood,
Nor yet a mountain nor a river sprite
A woman ye behold, most holy ones,
Whose moving story I will tell you true.
The Raja of Vidarbha is my sire,
Bhima his name, and - Best of Twice-born! - know
My husband is Nishadha's Chief, the famed,
The wise and valiant and victorious Prince,
The high and lordly Nala; of the gods
A steadfast worshipper; of Brahmanas
The friend his people's shield honored and strong,
Truth- speaking, skilled in arms, sagacious, just
Terrible to his foes, fortunate, lord
Of many conquered towns; a godlike man,
Princeliest of princes, - Nala, - one that hath
A countenance like the full moon's for light,
And eyes of lotus. This true offerer

Of sacrifices, this close votary
Of Vedas and Vedângas, in the war
Deadly to enemies, like sun and moon
For splendor, - by some certain evil ones
Being defied to dice, my virtuous prince
Was, by their wicked acts, of realm despoiled,
Wealth, jewels, all. I am his woful wife.
The Princess Damayanti. Seeking him
Through thickets have I roamed, over rough hills,
By crag and river and the reedy lake,
By marsh and waterfall and jungle-bush,
In quest of him, -my lord, my warrior,
My hero, - and still roam, uncomforted.
Worshipful Brethren! say if he hath come,
Nishadha's Chief, my Nala, hitherward
Unto your pleasant homes, -he, for whose sake
I wander in the dismal pathless wood
With bears and tigers haunted -terrible?
Ah! if I find him not, ere there be passed
Many more nights and days, peace will I win;
For death shall set my mournful spirit free.
What cause have I to live, lacking my Prince?
Why should I longer breathe, whose heart is dead
With sorrow for my lord?"

To Bhima's child,
So in the wood bewailing, made reply
Those holy, truthful men: "Beautiful One
The future is for thee; fair will it fall!
Our eyes, by long devotions opened, see
Even now - thy lord - thou shalt behold him soon,
Nishadha's chief, the famous Nala, strong
In battle, loving justice. Yea, this Prince
Thou wilt regain, Bhima's sad daughter! freed
From troubles, purged of sin; and witness him -
With all his gems and glories - governing
Nishadha once again, invincible,
joy of his friends and terror of his foes.
Yea, Noblest, thou shalt have thy love anew
In days to come."

So speaking, from the sight
Of Damayanti, at that instant, passed
Hermits, with hermitage and holy fires,
Evanishing. In wonderment she stood,
Gazing bewildered. Then the Princess cried:
"Was it in dream I saw them? Whence befell
This unto me? Where are the brethren gone,
The ring of huts, the pleasant stream that ran
With birds upon its crystal banks, the grove
Delightful, with its fruits and flowers?" Long whilc
Pondered and wondered Damayanti there,
Her bright smile fled, pale, strengthless, sorrowful
Then to another region of the wood,
With sighs, and eyes welling great tears, she passed,
Lamenting - till a beauteous tree she spied, -
The Asoka, best of trees. Fair rose it there
Beside the forest, glowing with the flame
Of golden and crimson blossoms, and its boughs
Full of sweet-singing birds.

"Ahovat, - Look!"
She cried: "Ah, lovely tree, that wavest here
Thy crown of countless, shining, clustering blooms
As thou wert woodland king, - Asoka tree,
Tree called 'the sorrow-ender,' heart's-ease tree
Be what thy name saith, - end my sorrow now,
Saying, ah, bright Asoka! thou hast seen
My Prince, my dauntless Nala; seen that lord
Whom Damayanti loves and his foes fear;
Seen great Nishadha's Chief, so dear to me,
His tender princely skin in rended cloth
Scantily clad. Hath he passed wandering
Under thy branches, grievously forlorn?
Answer, Asoka! 'Sorrow-ender,' speak
That I go sorrowless, O heart's-ease, be
Truly heart's-easing, - ease my heart of pain."[1]

---

[1] The translation here repeats the play of words in the original: Satyanâmâ
bhawâsoka, asoka sokanâshana.

Thus, wild with grief, she spake unto the tree,
Round and round walking, as to reverence it;
And then, unanswered, the sweet lady sped
Though wastes more dreadful, passing many a ran,
Many still-gliding rillets, many a peak

Tree-clad, with beasts and birds of wondrous kind,
In dark ravines, and caves, and lonely glooms.
These things saw Damayanti, Bhima's child,
Seeking her lord.

At last, on the long road,
She, whose soft smile was once so beautiful,
A caravan encountered. Merchantmen
With trampling horses, elephants, and wains,
Made passage of a river, running slow
In cool, clear waves. The quiet waters gleamed,
Shining and wide outspread, between the canes
Which bordered it, wherefrom echoed the cries
Of fish-hawks, curlews, and red chakravâks,
With sounds of leaping fish and water-snakes,
And tortoises, amid its shoals and flats
Sporting or feeding.

When she spied that throng,
Heart-maddened with her anguish, weak and wan,
Half clad, bloodless and thin, her long black locks
Matted with dust, - breathlessly brake she in
Upon them, - Nala's wife, - so beauteous once,
So honored. Seeing her, some fled in fear
Some gazed, speechless with wonder; some called out,
Mocking the piteous face by words of scorn
But some (my King!) had pity of her woe,
And spake her fair, inquiring: "Who art thou?
And whence? And in this grove what seekest thou,
To come so wild? Thy mien astonisheth.
Art of our kind, or art thou something strange,
The spirit of the forest, or the hill,
Or river valley? Tell us true - then we

Will buy thy favor. If, indeed, thou be'st
Yakshini,. Rakshasi, or she-creature
Haunting this region, be propitious! Send
Our caravan in safety on its path,
That we may quickly, by thy fortune, go
Homeward, and all fair chances fall to us."

Hereby accosted, softly gave response
That royal lady, - weary for her lord,-
Answering the leader of the caravan,
And those that gathered round, a marvelling throng
Of men and boys and elders: "Oh, believe
I am as you, of mortal birth, but born
A Raja's child, and made a Raja's wife.
Him seek I, Chieftain of Nishadha, named
Prince Nala, - famous, glorious, first in war.
If ye know aught of him, my king, my joy,
My tiger of the jungle, my lost lord,
Quick, tell me, comfort me!"

Then one who led
Their line, - the merchant Suchi, - answering,
Spake to the peerless Princess: "Hear me now.
I am the captain of this caravan,
But nowhere any named by Nala's name
Have I, or these, beheld. Of evil beasts
The woods were full, - cheetahs and bears and cats,
Tigers and elephants, bison and boar;
Those saw we in the brake on every side,
But nowhere nought of human shape, save thee.
May Manibhadra, have us in his grace, -
The Lord of Yakshas, - as I tell thee truth!"

Then sadly spake she to the trader-chief
And to his band: "Whither wend ye, I pray?
Please ye, acquaint me where this Sarthâ[1] goes."

Replied the captain: "Unto Chedi's realm,

---

[1] A caravan.

Where rules the just Subâhu, journey we,
To sell our merchandise, daughter of men!"

THUS by the chieftain of the band informed,
The peerless Princess journeyed with them, still
Seeking her lord. And at the first the way
Fared through another forest, dark and deep
Afterwards came the traders to a pool
Broad, everywhere delightful, odorous

With cups of opened lotus, and its shores
Green with rich grass, and edged with garden-trees,-
A place of flowers and fruits and singing birds.
So cool and clear and peacefully, it gleamed,
That men and cattle, weary with the march,
Clamored to pitch; and, on their chieftain's sign,
The pleasant hollow entered they, and camped
All the long caravan - at sunset's hour.

There, in the quiet of the middle night,
Deep slumbered these; when, sudden on them fell
A herd of elephants, thirsting to drink,
In rut, the mada[1] oozing from their heads.
And when those great beasts spied the caravan,
And smelled the tame cows of their kind, they rushed
Headlong, and, mad with must,[2] o'erwhelming all,

WIth onset vast and irresistible.
As when from some tall peak into the plain
Thunder and smoke and crash the rolling rocks,
Through splintered sterns and thorns breaking their path,
So swept the herd to where, beside the pool,
Those sleepers lay; and tram pled them to earth
Half-risen, helpless, shrieking in the dark-,
"Haha! the elephants!" Of those unslain,
Some in the thickets sought a shelter; some,

---

[1] This is a secretion which flows by a small orifice from the elephant's temples at
certain seasons. It is sweet-smelling, and constantly alluded to in Hindoo poetry.
[2] The Indian word for the condition described.

Yet dazed with sleep, stood panic-stricken, mute;
Till here with tusks, and there with trunks, the beasts
Gored them, and battered them, and trod them flat
Under their monstrous feet. Then might be seen
Camels with camel-drivers perishing,
And men flying in fear, who struck at men,
Terror and death and clamor everywhere:
While some, despairing, cast themselves to earth;
And some, in fleeing, fell and died; and some
Climbed to the tree-tops. Thus on every side
Scattered and ruined was that caravan, -
Cattle and merchants, - by the herd assailed.
So hideous was the tumult, all three worlds
Seemed filled with fright; and one was heard to cry
"The fire is in the tents! fly for your lives!
Stay not!" And others cried: "Look where we
Our treasures trodden down; gather them! Halt
Why run ye, losing ours and yours? Nay, stay!
Stand ye, and we will stand!" And then to these
One voice cried, "Stand!" another, "Fly! we die!"
Answered by those again who shouted, "Stand!
Think what we lose, O cowards!"

While this rout
Raged, amid dying groans and sounds of fear,
The Princess, waking startled, terror-struck,
Saw such a sight as might the boldest daunt, -
Such scene as those great lovely lotus-eyes
Ne'er gazed upon before. Sick with new dread, -
Her breath suspended 'twixt her lips, - she rose
And heard, of those surviving, some one moan
Amidst his fellows: "From whose evil act
Is this the fruit? Hath worship not been paid
To mighty Manibhadra? Gave we not
The reverence due to Vaishravan, that King
Of all the Yakshas? Was not offering made
At outset to the spirits which impede?
Is this the evil portent of the birds?
Were the stars adverse? or what else hath fall'n?

And others said, wailing for friends and goods:
"Who was that woman, with mad eyes, that came
Into our camp, ill-favored, hardly cast
In mortal mould? By her, be sure, was wrought
This direful sorcery. Demon or witch,
Yakshi or Rakshasi, or gliding ghost,
Or something frightful, was she. Hers this deed
Of midnight murders; doubt there can be none.
Ah, if we could espy that hateful one,
The ruin of our march, the woe-maker,
With stones, clods, canes, or clubs, nay, with clenched fists,
We 'd strike her dead, the murderess of our band!"

Trembling the Princess heard those angry words;
And - saddened, maddened, shamed - breathless she fled
Into the thicket, doubtful if such sin
Might not be hers, and with fresh dread distressed.
"Aho!" she weeps, "pitiless grows the wrath
Of Fate against me. Not one gleam of good
Arriveth. Of what fault is this the fruit?
I cannot call to mind a wrong I wrought
To any - even a little thing - in act
Or thought or word; whence then hath come this curse?
Belike from ill deeds done in bygone lives
It hath befall'n, and what I suffer now
Is payment of old evils undischarged.[1]
Grievous the doom, - my palace lost, my lord,
My children, kindred; I am torn'away

From home and love and all, to roam accurst
In this plague-haunted waste!"

When brake the day,
Those which escaped alive, with grievous cries
Departed, mourning for their fellows slain.
Each one a kinsman or a friend laments,
Father or brother, son, or comrade dear.

---

[1] This anticipation of the Buddhist doctrine of Karma is very curious.

And Damayanti, hearing, weeps anew,
Saying: "What dreadful sin was that I wrought
Long, long ago, which, when I chance to meet
These wayfarers in the unpeopled wood,
Dooms them to perish by the elephants,
In my dark destiny enwrapped? No doubt
More and more sorrow I shall bear, or bring,
For none dies ere his time; this is the lore
Of ancient sages; this is why -being glad
If I could die - I was not trampled down
Under the elephants. There haps to man
Nothing unless by destiny. Why else,
Seeing that never have I wrought one wrong,
From childhood's hours, in thought or word or deed,
Hath this woe chanced? May be - meseerns it may!-
The mighty gods, at my Swayamvara
Slighted by me for Nala's dearest sake,
Are wroth, and by their dread displeasure thus
To loss and loneliness I am consigned!"

So - woe-begone and wild - this noble wife,
Deserted Damayanti, poured her griefs:
And afterwards, with certain Brahmanas
Saved from the rout, - good men who knew the Veds,
Sadly her road she finished, like the moon
That goeth clouded in the month of rain.
Thus travelling long, the Princess drew at last
Nigh to a city, at the evening hour.
The dwelling-place it was of Chedi's Chief,
The just Subâhu. Through its lofty gates
Painfully passed she, clad in half a cloth;
And as she entered, - sorrow-stricken, wan,
Foot-weary, stained with mire, with unsmoothed hair-,
Unbathed, and eyes of madness, - those who saw,
Wondered and stared, and watched her as she toiled
Down the long city-street. The children brake
From play, and -boys with girls - followed her steps,
So that she came - a crowd encompassing -
Unto the King's door. On the palace roof
The mother of the Maharaja paced,

And marked the throng, and that sad wayfarer.
Then to her nurse spake the queen-mothcr this
"Go thou, and bring yon woman unto me!
The people trouble her; mournful she walks,
Seeming unfriended, yet bears she a mien
Made for a king's abode, and, all so wild,
Still are her wistful eyes like the great eyes
Of Lakshmi's self." So downwards went the nurse,
Bidding the rude folk back; and to the roof
Of the great palace led that wandering one,
Desolate Damayanti, -whom the Queen
Courteous besought: "Though thou art wan of face,
Thou wear'st a noble air, which through thy griefs
Shineth as lightning doth behind its cloud.
Tell me thy name, and whose thou art, and whencc.
No low-born form is thine, albeit thou com'st
Wearing no ornaments; and all alone
Wanderest, - not fearing men, -by some spell safe."

Hearing which words, the child of Bhima spake
Gratefully this: "A woful woman I,
And woful wife, but faithful to my vows;
High-born, but like a servant, like a slave,
Lodging where it may hap, and finding food
From the wild roots and fruits wherever night
Brings me my resting-place. Yet is my lord
A prince noble and great, with countless gifts
Endued; and him I followed faithfully
As 'twere his shadow, till hard fate decreed
That he should fall into the rage of dice
And, worsted in that play, into the wood
He fled, clad in one cloth, frenzied and lone.
And I his steps attended in the wood,
Comforting him, my husband. But it chanccd,
Hungry and desperate, he lost his cloth;
And I - one garment bearing - followed still
My unclad lord, despairing, reasonless,
Through many a weary night not slumbering.
But when, at length, a little while I slept,
My Prince abandoned me, rending away

Half of my garment, leaving there his wife,
Who never wrought him wrong. That lord I seek
By day and night, with heart and soul on fire, -
Seek, but still find not; though he is to me
Brighter than light which gleams from lotus-cups,
Divine as are the immortals, dear as breath,
The master of my life, my pride, my joy!"

Whom, grieving so, her sweet eyes blind with tears,
Gently addressed Subâhu's mother, - sad
To hear as she to tell. "Stay with us here,
Thou ill-starred lady. Great the friendliness
I have for thee. The people of our court
Shall thy lost husband seek; or, it may be,
He too will wander hither of himself
By devious paths: yea, mournful one, thy lord
Thou wilt regain, abiding with us here."

And Damayanti, bowing, answered thus
Unto the Queen: "I will abide with thee,
O mother of illustrious sons, if so
They feed me not on orts, nor seek from me
To wash the feet of comers, nor that I
Be set to speak with any stranger-men
Before the curtain; and, if any man
Sue me, that he be punished; and if twice,
Then that he die, guilty of infamy.
This is my earnest prayer; but Brahmanas
Who seek my husband, or bear news of him,
Such will I speak with. If it may be thus,
Gladly would I abide, great lady, here;
If otherwise, it is not on my mind
To sojourn longer."

Very tenderly
Quoth the queen-mother: "All that thou dost ask
We will ordain. The gods reward thy love,
Which hath such honor!" Comforting her so,
To the king's daughter, young Sunandâ, spake
The -Maharajni: "See, Sunandâ, here

Clad as a handmaid, but in form divine,
One of thy years, gentle and true. Be friends;
Take and give pleasure in glad company
Each with the other, keeping happy hearts."

So went Sunandâ joyous to her house,
Leading with loving hand the Princess in,
The maidens of the court accompanying.

Part Two

NOT long (O Maharaj!) was Nala fled
From Damayanti, when, in midmost gloom
Of the thick wood a flaming fire he spied,
And from the fire's heart heard proceed a voice
Of one imperilled, crying many times:
"Haste hither, Punyashloka,[1] Nala, haste!"
"Fear not," the Prince replied; "I come and sprang
Across the burning bushes, where he saw
A snake - a king of serpents - lying curled
In a great ring, which reared its dancing crest
Saluting, and in human accents spoke:
"Maharaj, kindly lord, I am the snake
Karkôtaka; by me was once betrayed
The famous Rishi Narada; his wrath
Doomed me, thou Chief of men! to bear this spell.

'Coil thy false folds,' said he, 'forever here,
A serpent, motionless upon this spot,
'Fill it shall chance that Nala passeth by
And bears thee hence; then only from my curse
Canst thou be freed.' And prisoned by that curse
I have no power to stir, though the wood burns
Nay, not a coil! good fellowship I'll show
If thou wilt succor me. I'll be to thee
A faithful friend, as no snake ever yet.
Lift me, and quickly from the flames bear forth:
For thee I shall grow light." Thereat shrank up

---

[1] "Praised-in-song."

That monstrous reptile to a finger's length;
And grasping this, unto a place secure
From burning, Nala bore it, where the air
Breathed freshly, and the fire's black path was stayed.

Then made the Prince to lay the serpent down,
But yet again it speaks: "Nishadha's Lord,
Grasp me and slowly go, counting thy steps;
For, Raja, thou shalt have good fortune hence."
So Nala slowly went, counting his steps;
And when the tenth pace came, the serpent turned
And bit the Prince. No sooner pierced that tooth
Than all the likeness of Nishadha changed;
And, wonder-struck, he gazed upon himself,
While from the dust he saw the snake arise
A man, and, speaking as Karkôtaka,
Comfort him thus:-

"Thou art by me transformed
That no man know thee and that evil one
(Possessing, and undoing thee, with grief)
Shall so within thee by my venom smart,
Shall through thy blood so ache, that - till he quit
He shall endure the woe he did impart.
Thus by my potent spell, most noble Prince
(Who sufferest too long) thou wilt be freed
From him that haunts thee. Fear no more the wood,
Thou tiger of all princes! fear thou not
Horned nor fanged beasts, nor any enemies,
Though they be Brahmans! safe thou goest now,
Guarded from grief and hurt, - Chieftain of men
By this kind poison. In the fields of war
Henceforth the victory always falls to thee
Go joyous, therefore, Prince - give thyself forth
For 'Vahûka, the charioteer:' repair
To Rituparna's city, who is skilled
In play, and dwells in fair Ayodhyâ.
Wend thou, Nishadha! thither; he will teach
Great subtlety in numbers unto thee,
Exchanging this for thine own matchless gift

Of taming horses. From the lordly line
Descended of Ikshvaku,[1] glad and kind
The King will be; and thou, learning of him
His deepest act of dice, wilt win back all,
And clasp again thy Princess. Therefore waste
No thought on woes. I tell thee truth! thy realm
Thou shalt regain; and when the time is come
That thou hast need to put thine own form on,

Call me to mind, O Prince, and tie this cloth
Around thy body. Wearing it, thy shape
Thou shalt resume."

Therewith the serpent gave
A magic twofold robe, not wove on earth,
Which (O thou son of Kuru!) Nala took;
And so the snake, transformed, vanished away.

THE great snake being gone, Nishadha's Chief
Set forth, and on the tenth day entered in
At Rituparna's town; there he besought
The presence of the Raja, and spake thus
"I am the chariot-driver, Vahûka.
There is not on this earth another man
Hath gifts like mine to tarne and guide the steed
Moreover, thou mayst use me in nice needs
And dangerous, where kings lack faithful hearts.
Specially seen I am in dressing meats; [2]

And whatso other duties may befall,
Though they be weighty, I shall execute,
If, Rituparna, thou wilt take me in."

"I take thee," quoth the King. "Dwell here with me.
Such service as thou knowest, render us.
'Tis, Vahûka, forever in my heart

----

[1] The first monarch of the Solar Dynasty.
[2] This, it will be remembered, was one of the divine gifts bestowed upon Nala after
the Swayamvara.

To have my steeds the swiftest; be thy task
To train me horses like the wind for speed;
My charioteer I make thee, and thy wage
Ten thousand gold suvernas. Thou wilt have
For fellows, Varshneya and Jîvala;
With those abiding, lodge thou happy here."

So entertained and honored of the King,
In Rituparna's city Nala dwelled,
Lodging with Varshneya and Jîvala.

There sojourned he, (my Raja!) thinking still
Of sweet Vidarbha's Princess day by -day;
And sunset after sunset one sad strain
He sang: "Where resteth she that roamed the wood
Hungry and parched and worn, but always true?
Doth she remember yet her faultful lord?
Ah, who is near her now?" So it befell
Jivala heard him ever sighing this,
And questioned: "Who is she thou dost lament?
Say, Vahûka! fain would I know her name.
Long life be thine; but tell me who he is,
The faultful man that was the lady's lord."

And Nala answered him: "There lives a man,
Evil and rash, that had a noble wife.
False to his word he was; and thus it fell
That somewhere, for some reason, (ask not me!)
He quitted her, this rash one. And - so wrenched
Apart from hers - his spirit, bad and sad,
Muses and moans, with grief's slow fire consumed
Night-time and day-time. Thence it is he sings
At every sunset this unchanging verse,
An outcast on the earth, by hazard led
Hither or thither. Such a man thou seest
Woful, unworthy, holding in his heart
Always that sin. I was that lady's lord,
Whom she did follow through the dreadful wood,
Living by me abandoned, at this hour;
If yet, in truth, she lives, - youthful, alone,

Unpractised in the ways, not meriting
Fortunes so hard. Ah, if, indeed, she lives,
Who roamed the thick and boundless forest, full
Of prowling beasts, -roamed it, my Jivala,
Unguarded by her guilty lord, - forsook,
Betrayed, good friend!"

Thus did Nishadha grieve,
Calling sweet Damayanti to his mind.
So tarried he within the Raja's house,
And no man knew his place of sojourning.

WHILE, stripped of state, the Prince and Princess thus,
Were sunk to servitude, Bhima made quest,
Sending his Brahmans forth to search for them
With strait commands, and for their road-money
Liberal store. "Seek everywhere," said he
Unto the twice-born, "Nala, - everywhere
My daughter Damayanti. Whoso comes
Successful in this quest, discovering her, -
With lost Nishadha's Lord, - and bringing them,
A thousand cows to that man will I give,
And village-lands whence shall be revenue
As great as from a city. If so be
Ye cannot bring me Nala and my child,
To him that learns their refuge I will give
The thousand cows."

Thereby rejoiced, they went,
Those Brahmans, hither and thither, up and down,
Into all regions, rajaships, and towns,
Seeking Nishadha's Chieftain, and his wife.
But Nala nowhere found they; nowhere found
Sweet Damayanti, Bhima's beauteous child.

Until, straying to pleasant Chedipur,
One day a twice-born came, Sudêva named,
And entered in; and, spying round about
(Upon a feast-day by the King proclaimed),
He saw forth-passing through the palace-gate

A woman, - Bhima's daughter, - side by side
With young Sunandâ. Little praise had now
That beauty which in old days shone so bright;
Marred with much grief it was, like sunlight dimmed
By fold on fold of wreathed and creeping mists.
But when Sudêva marked the great dark eyes,
Lustreless though they were, and she so worn,
So listless, - "Lo, the Princess!" whispered he;
"'Tis the King's daughter," quoth he to himself;
And thus mused on: -

"Yea! as I used to see,
'Tis she! no other woman hath such grace
My task is done; I gaze on that one form,
Which is like Lakshmi's, whom all worlds adore.
I see the bosoms, rounded, dark, and smooth,
As they were sister-moons - the soft moon-face
Which with its queenly light makes all things bright
Where it doth gleam; the large deep lotus-eyes,
That, like to Rati's own, the Queen of Love,
Beam, each a lovelit star, filling the worlds
With longing. Ah, fair lotus-flower, plucked up
By Fate's hard grasp from far Vidarbha's pool,
How is thy cup muddied and slimed to-day!
Ah, moon, how is thy night like to the eclipse
When Rahu swallows up the silver round!
Ah, tearless eyes, reddened with weeping him,
How are ye like to gentle streams run dry
Ah, lake of lilies, where grief's elephant
Hath swung his trunk, and turned the crystal black,
And scattered all the blue and crimson cups,
And frightened off the birds! Ah, lily-cup,
Tender, and delicately leaved, and reared
To blossom in a palace built of gems,
How dost thou wither here, wrenched by the root,
Sun-scorched and faded! Noblest, loveliest, best
Who bear'st no gems, yet so becomest them, -
How like the new moon's silver horn thou art,
When envious black clouds blot it! Lost for thee
Are love, home, children, friends, and kinsmen; lost

All joy of that fair body thou dost wear
Only that it may last to find thy lord.
Truly a woman's ornament is this:
The husband is her jewel; lacking him
She hath none, though she shines with priceless pearls;
Piteous must be her state! And, torn from her,
Doth Nala cling to life; or, day by day,
Waste with long yearning. Oh, as I behold
Those black locks, and those eyes, - dark and long-shaped
As are the hundred-petalled lotus-leaves, -
And watch her joyless who deserves all joy,
My heart is sore! When will she overpass
The river of this sorrow, and come safe
Unto its farther shore? When will she meet
Her lord, as moon and moon-star [1] in the sky
Mingle? For, as I think, in winning her,
Nala would win his happy days again,
And - albeit banished now - have back his lands.
Alike in years and graces, and alike
In lordly race these were: no bride could seem
Worthy Nishadha, if it were not she;
Nor husband worthy of Vidarbha's Pride,
Save it were Nala. It is meet I bring
Comfort forthwith to yon despairing one,
The consort of the just and noble Prince,
For whom I see her heart-sick. I will go
And speak good tidings to this moon-faced Queen,
Who once knew nought of sorrows, but to-day
Stands yonder, plunged heart-deep in woful thought."

So, all those signs and marks considering
Which stamped her Bhima's child, Sudêva drew

Nearer, and said: "Vidarbhi, Nala's wife,
I am the Brahmana Sudêva, friend
Unto my lord, thy brother, and I come
By royal Bhima's mandate seeking thee.
That Maharaj, thy father, dwells in health

---

[1] Rohini, the fourth lunar asterism.

Thy mother and thy house are well; and well -
With promise of long years -thy little ones,
Sister and brother. Yet, for thy sake, Queen,
Thy kindred sit as men with spirit gone -
In search of thee a hundred twice-born rove
Over all lands."

But (O King Yudhisthir!)
Hardly one word she heard before she broke
With question after question on the man,
Asking of this dear friend and that and this;
All mingled with quick tears, and tender sighs,
And hungry gazing on her brother's friend,
Sudêva - best of Brahmanas - come there.
Which soon Sunandâ marked, watching them speak
Apart, and Damayanti all in tears.
Then came she to her mother, saying: "See,
The handmaid thou didst give me talks below
With one who is a Brahman, all her words
Watered with weeping; if thou wilt, demand
What this man knows."

Therewith swept forth amazed
The mother of the Raja, and beheld
How Nala's wife spake with the Brahmana.
Whom straight she bade them summon; and, being brought,
In this wise questioned: "Knowest thou whose wife,
Whose daughter, this one is; and how she left
Her kin; and wherefore, being heavenly-eyed
And noble-mannered, she hath wandered here?
I am full fain to hear this; tell me all,
No whit withholding; answer faithfully.
Who is our slave-girl with the goddess gait?
The Brahmana Sudêva, so addressed,
Seating himself at ease, unto the Queen
Told Damayanti's story, how all fell.

SUDÊVA said: "There reigns in majesty
King Bhima at Vidarbha; and of him
The Princess Damayanti here is child;

And Virasena's son, Nala, is Lord
Over Nishadha, praised-in-song and wise;
And of that Prince this lady is the wife.
In play his brother worsted Nala; stripped
Of lands and wealth the Prince; who fled his realm,
Wandering with Damayanti, -where, none knew.
In quest of Damayanti we have roamed
The earth's face o'er, until I found her here
In thy son's house, the King's, - the very same,
Since like to her for grace no woman fives
Of all fair women. Where her eyebrows meet
A pretty mole, born with her, should be seen
A little lotus-bud - not visible
By reason of the dust of toil which clouds
Her face and veils its moonlike beauty - that
The wondrous Maker [1] on the rare work stamped
To be His mark. But as the waxing moon
Goes thin and darkling for a while, then rounds
The crescent's rims with splendors, so this Queen
Hath lost not queenliness. Being now obscured,
Soiled with the grime of chores, unbeautified,
She shows true gold. The fire which trieth gold
Denoteth less itself by instant heat
Than Damayanti by her goodlihood.
At first sight knew I her. She bears that mole."

Whilst yet Sudêva spake, (O King of men!)
Sunandâ from the slave's front washed away
The gathered dust, and forth that mark appeared
'Twixt Damayanti's brows, as when clouds break,
And in the sky the moon, the night-maker, [2]

Glittcrs to view. Seeing the spot awhile,
Sunandâ and the mother of the King
Gazed voiceless; then they clasped her neck and wcpt
Rejoicing, till the Queen, staying her tears,
Exclaimed: "My sister's daughter, dear! thou art,

---

[1] The Sanskrit word is Dhâtri.
[2] The Sanskrit epithet is Nisâkara.

By this same mark. Thy mother and myself
Were sisters by one father, - he that rules
Dasarna, King Sudâman. She was given
To Bhima, and to Virabahu I.
Once at Dasarna, in my father's house,
I saw thee, newly born. Thy race and mine,
Princess, are one: henceforward, therefore, here
As I am, Damayanti, shalt thou be."

With gladdened heart did Damayanti bend
Before her mother's sister, answering thus:
"Peaceful and thankful dwelled I here with thee,
Being unknown, my every need supplied,
My life and honor by thy succor safe,
Yet, Maharajni, even than this dear home
One would be dearer: 'tis so many days
Since we were parted. Suffer me to go
Where those my tender little ones were led;
So long - poor babes ! - of me and of their sire
Bereft. If, lady, thou dost think to show
Kindness to me, this is my wish: to wend
Unto Vidarbha swiftly; wilt thou bid
They bear me thither?"

Was no sooner heard
That fond desire, than the queen-mother gave
Willing command; and soon an ample troop,
The King consenting, gathered for her guard.
So was she sent upon a palanquin,
With soldiers, pole-bearers, and meat and drink,
And garments as befitted - happier - home.

Thus to Vidarbha came its Pride again,
By no long road; and joyously her kin
Brought the sweet Princess in, and welcomed her.
In peace and safety all her house she found
Her children well; - father and mother, friends.
The gods she worshipped, and to Brahmanas
Due reverence made, and whatso else was meet
That Damayanti did, regal in all.

To wise Sudêva fell the thousand cows
By Bhima granted, with the village-lands,
And goodly gifts beside.

But when there passed
One night of rest within the palace-walls,
The wistful Princess to her mother said:
"If thou wouldst have me live, I tell thee true,
Dear mother, it must be by bringing back
My Nala, my own lord; and only so."

When this she spake, right sorrowful became
The Rani, weeping silently, nor gave
One word of answer; and the palace-girls,
Seeing this grief, sat round them, weeping too,
And crying: "Haha! where is gone her lord?
And loud the lamentation was of all.

Afterwards to the Maharaj his Queen
Told what was said: "Lord! all uncomforted
Thy daughter Damayanti weeps and grieves,
Lacking her husband. E'ven to me she spake
Before our damsels, laying shame aside
'Find Nala - let the people of the cotirt
Strive day and night to learn where Nala is.'

Then Bhima, hearing, called his Brahmanas
Patient and wise, and issued hest to go
Into all regions, seeking for the Prince.
But first, by mandate of the Maharaj,
To Damayanti all those twice-born came,
Saying: "Now we depart!" Then Bhima's child
Gave ordinance: "To whatsoever lands
Ye wend, say this, - wherever gather men,
Say this, - in every place these verses speak:-

Whither art thou departed, cruel lover,
Who stole the half of thy belovèd's cloth,
And left her to awaken, and discover
The wrong thou wroughtest to the love of both?

She, as thou didst command, a sad watch keepeth,
With woful heart wearing the rended dress.
Prince, hear her cry who thus forever weepeth:
Be mindful, hero; comfort her distress!

And, furthermore, "the Princess said," since fire
Leaps into flame when the wind fans the spark,
Be this too spoken, that his heart may burn: -

By every husband nourished and protected
Should every wife be. Think upon the wood!
Why these thy duties hast thou so neglected,
Prince, that wast callèd noble and true and good?

Art then become compassionate no longer,
Shunning, perchance, my fortune's broken way?
Ah, husband, love is most! let love be stronger;
Ahimsa paro dharma,[1] thou didst say.

These verses while ye speak," quoth the Princess,
"Should any man make answer, note him well
In any place; and who he is, and where
He dwells. And if one listens to these words
Intently, and shall so reply to them,
Good Brahmans, hold ye fast his speech, and bring
Breath by breath, all of it unto me here;
But so that he shall know not whence ye speak,
If ye go back. Do this unweariedly;
And if one answer, - be he high or low,
Wealthy or poor, - learn all he was and is,
And what he would."

Hereby enjoined, they went,
Those twice-born, into all the lands to seek
Prince Nala in his loneliness. Through towns,

Cities and villages, hamlets and camps,

---

[1] "Gentleness is chief of virtues."

By shepherds' huts and hermits' caves, they passed,
Searching for Nala; yet they found him not
Albeit in every region (O my king!)
The words of Damayanti, as she taught,
Spake they again in hearing of all men.

SUDDENLY - after many days - there came
A Brahman back, Parnâda he was called,
Who unto Bhima's child in this wise spake:
O Damayanti, seeking Nala still,
Ayodhyâ's streets I entered, where I saw
The Maharaj; he - noble-minded one! -
Heard me thy verses say, as thou hadst said;
Great Rituparna heard those very words,
Excellent Princess; but he answered nought;
And no man answered, out of all the throng
Ofttimes addressed. But when I had my leave
And was withdrawn, a man accosted me
Privately, - one of Rituparna's train,
Vâhuka named, the Raja's charioteer
(Something misshapen, with a shrunken arm,
But skilled in driving, very dexterous
In cookery and sweetmeats). He -with groans,
And tears which rolled and rolled - asked of my health,
And then these verses spake full wistfully: -

Even when their loss is largest, noble ladies
Keep the true treasure of their hearts unspent,
Attaining heaven through faith, which undismayed is
By wrong, unaltered by abandonment;

Such an one guards with virtue's golden shield
Her name from harm; pious and pure and tender;
And, though her lord forsook her, will not yield
To wrath, even against that vile offender,-

Even against the ruined, rash, ungrateful,
Faithless, fond Prince from whom the birds did steal
His only cloth, whom now a penance fateful
Dooms to sad days, that dark-eyed will not feel

Anger; for if she saw him she should see
A man consumed with grief and loss and shame;
Ill or well lodged, ever in misery,
Her unthroned lord, a slave without a name.

Such words I heard him speak," Parnâda said,
"And, hastening thence, I tell them to thee, here
Thou knowest; thou wilt judge; make the King know."

But Damayanti listened, with great eyes
Welling quick tears, while thus Parnâda spake,
And afterwards crept secretly and said
Unto her mother: "Breathe no word hereof,
Dear mother, to the King, but let me speak
With wise Sudêva in thy presence here;
Nothing should Bhima know of what I plan,
But, if thou lovest me, by thee and me
This shall be wrought. As I was safely led
By good Sudêva home, so let him go -
With not less happy fortune - to bring back,
Ere many days, my Nala; let him seek
Ayodhyâ, mother dear, and fetch my Prince!"

But first Parnâda, resting from his road, -
That best of twice-borns, - did the Princess thank
With honorable words and gifts: "If home
My Nala cometh, Brahman!" so she spake,
"Great guerdon will I give. Thou hast well done
For me herein, - better than any man;
Helping me find again my wandered lord."
To which fair words made soft reply, and prayers
For "peace and fortune," that high-minded one,
And so passed home, his service being wrought.

Next to Sudêva spake the sad Princess
This, (O my King!) her mother standing by:
"Good Brahman, to Ayodhyâ's city go.
Say in the ears of Raja Rituparn,
As though thou cam'st a simple traveller,'

'The daughter of King Bhima once again
Maketh to hold her high Swayamvara.
The kings and princes from all lands repair
Thither the time draws nigh; to-morrow', dawn
Shall bring the day. If thou wouldst be of it,
Speed quickly, conquering King! at sunsetting
Another lord she chooseth for herself;
Since whether Nala liveth or is dead,
None knoweth.'"

These the words which he should say;
And, learning them, he sped, and thither came, -
That Brahmana. Sudêva, - and he spake
To Maharaja Rituparna so.[1]

Now when the Raja Rituparna heard
Sudêva's words, quoth he to Vâhuka
Full pleasantly: "Much mind I have to go
Where Damayanti holds Swayamvara,
If to Vidarbha, in a single day,
Thou deenicst we might drive, my charioteer!"

Of Nala, by his Raja thus addressed,
Tom was the heart with anguish; for he thought:
"Can Damayanti purpose this? Could grief
So change her? Is it not some fine device
For my sake schemed? Or doth my Princess seek,
All holy as she was, this guilty joy,
Being so wronged of me, her rash weak lord?
Frail is a woman's heart, and my fault great!
Thus might she do it, being far from home,
Bereft of friends, desolate with long woes
Of love for me, - my slender-waisted one
Yet no, no, no! she would not, - she that is
My children's mother! Be it false or true,
Best shall I know in going; therefore now
The will of Rituparna must I serve."

---

[1] The Sanskrit word is Kamaga, the exact equivalent of "pleasure-tourist."

Thus pondering in his mind, the troubled Prince
With joined palms meekly to his master said
"I shall thy hest accomplish! I can drive
In one day, Raja, to Vidarbha's gates."

Then in the royal stables - steed by steed,
Stallions and mares, Vâhuka scanned them all,
By Rituparna prayed quickly to choose.
Slowly he picked four coursers, under-fleshed,
But big of bone and sinew; fetlocked well
For journeying; high-bred, heavy-framed; of blood
To match the best, yet gentle; blemish-free;
Broad in the jaw, with scarlet nostrils spread;
Bearing the Avarthas,[1] the ten true marks, -
Reared on the banks of Indus, swift as wind.

Which, when the Raja looked upon, he cried,
Half-wrathful: "What thing thinkest thou to do?
Wilt thou betray me? How should sorry beasts,
Lean-ribbed and ragged, take us all that way,
The long road we must swiftly travel hence?"

Vâhuka answered: "See on all these four
The ten sure marks: one curl upon each crest,
Two on the cheeks, two upon either flank,
Two on the breast, and on each crupper one.
These to Vidarbha - doubt it not - will go
Yet, Raja, if thou wilt have others, speak;
And I shall yoke them."

Rituparna said:
I know thou hast deep skill in stable-craft;
Yoke therefore such four coursers as thou wilt,
But quickly!"

Thus those horses, two by two,
High-mettled, spare, and strong, Prince Nala put

---

[1] These are spots where the hair curls round, as upon the crown of the human
head.

Under the bars; and when the car was hitched,
And eagerly the Raja made to mount,
At sign the coursers bent their knees, and lay
Along the earth. Then Nala, (O my King!)
With kindly voice cheering the gaunt bright steeds,
Loosed them, and grasped the reins, and bade ascend
Varshneya: so he started, headlong, forth.

At cry of Vâhuka the four steeds sprung
Into the air, as they would fly with him;
And when the Raja felt them, fleet as wind,
Whirling along, mute sat he and amazed;
And much Varshneya mused to hear and see
The thundering of those wheels; the fiery four
So lightly held; Vâhuka's matchless art.
"Is Mâtali, who driveth Indra's car,
Our charioteer? for all the marks of him
Are here! or Sâlihotra can this be,
The god of horses, knowing all their ways,
Who here in mortal form his greatness hides?
Or is it - can it be - Nala the Prince,
Nala the steed-tamer?" Thus pondered he:
"Whatever Nala knew this one doth know.
Alike the mastery seems of both; alike
I judge their years. If this man be not he,
Two Nalas are there in the world for skill.
They say there wander mighty powers on earth
In strange disguises, who, divinely sprung,
Veil themselves from us under human mould;
Bewilderment it brings me, this his shape
Misshapen, - from conclusion that alone
Withholds me; yet I wist not what to think,
In age and manner like, - and so unlike
In form! Else Vâhuka I must have deemed
Nala, with Nala's gifts."

So in his heart
Varshneya, watching, wondered, -being himself
The second charioteer. But Rituparn
Sat joyous with the speed, delightedly

Marking the driving of the Prince: the eyes
Attent; the hand so firm upon the reins
The skill so quiet, wise, and masterful
Great joy the Maharaja had to see.

By stream and mountain, woodland-path and pool,
Swiftly, like birds that skim in air, they sped;
Till, as the chariot plunged, the Raja saw
His shoulder-mantle falling to the ground;
And - loath to lose the robe - albeit so pressed,
To Nala cried he, "Let me take it up;
Check the swift horses, wondrous charioteer;
And bid Varshneya light, and fetch my cloth."
But Nala answered: "Far it lies behind;
A yojana already we have passed;
We cannot turn again to pick it up."

A little onward Rituparna saw
Within the wood a tall Myrobolan
Heavy with fruit; hereat, eager he cried
"Now, Vâhuka, my skill thou mayst behold
In the Arithmic. All arts no man knows;
Each hath his wisdom, but in one man's wit
Is perfect gift of one thin-, and not more.
From yonder tree how many leaves and fruits,
Think'st thou, lie fall'n there upon the earth?
Just one above a thousand of the leaves,
And one above a hundred of the fruits;
And on those two limbs hang, of dancing leaves,
Five crores exact; and shouldst thou pluck yon bough,
Together with their shoots, on those twain boughs
Swing twice a thousand nuts and ninety-five!"

Vâhuka checked the chariot wonderingly,
And answered: "Imperceptible to me
Is what thou boastest, slayer of thy foes
But I to proof will put it, hewing down
The tree, and, having counted, I shall know.
Before thine eyes the branches twain I'll lop:
How prove thee, Maharaja, otherwise,

Whether this be or be not? I will count
One by one - fruits and leaves - before thee, King;
Varshneya, for a space, can rein the steeds."

To him replied the Raja: "Time is none
Now to delay."

Vâhuka answered quick
(His own set purpose serving): "Stay this space,
Or by thyself drive on! The road is good,
The son of Vrishni will be charioteer!"

On that the Raja answered soothingly:
"There is not in the earth another man
That hath thy skill; and by thy skill I look
To reach Vidarbha, O thou steed-tamer!
Thou art my trust; make thou not hindrance now
Yet would I suffer, too, what thou dost ask,
If thou couldst surely reach Vidarbha's gate
Before yon sun hath sunk."

Nala replied:
"When I have counted those vibhîtak boughs,
Vidarbha I will reach; now keep thy word."

Ill pleased, the Raja said: "Halt then, and count!
Take one bough from the branch which I shall show,
And tell its fruits, and satisfy thy soul."

So leaping from the car -eager he shore
The boughs, and counted; and all wonder-struck
To Rituparna spake: "Lo, as thou saidst
So many fruits there be upon this bough!
Exceeding marvellous is this thy gift,
I burn to know such learning, how it comes."

Answered the Raja, for his journey fain:
My mind is quick with numbers, skilled to count;
I have the science."

Give it me, dear Lord!
Vâhuka cried: "teach me, I pray, this lore,
And take from me my skill in horse-tarning."
Quoth Rituparn - impatient to proceed
Yet of such skill desirous: "Be it so!
As thou hast prayed, receive my secret art,
Exchanging with me here thy mastery
Of horses."

Thereupon did he impart
His rules of numbers, taking Nala's too.

But wonderful! So soon as Nala knew
That hidden gift, the accursed Kali leapt
Forth from his breast, the evil spirit's mouth
Spewing the poison of Karkôtaka
Even as he issued. From the afflicted Prince
That bitter plague of Kali passed away;
And for a space Prince Nala lost himself,
Rent by the agony. But when he saw
The evil one take visible shape again, -
Free from the serpent's poison, - Nishadh's Lord
Had thought to curse him then; but Kali stood
With clasped palms, trembling, and besought the Prince.
Saying: "Thy wrath restrain, Sovereign of men
I will repay thee well. Thy virtuous wife,
Indrasen's angered mother, laid her ban
Upon me when thou didst forsake her; since
Within thee have I dwelled in anguish sore,
Tortured and tossed and burning, night and day,
With venom from the great snake's fang, which passed
Into me by thy blood. Be pitiful!
I take my refuge in thy mercy! Hear
My promise, Prince! Wherever men henceforta
Shall name thee before people, praising thee,
This shall protect them from the dread of me;
NALA shall guard from KALI, if so now
Thou spare to curse me, seeking grace of thee."

Thus supplicated, Nala stayed his wrath,

Acceding; and the direful Kali fled
Into the Wounded tree, possessing it.
But of no eyes, save Nala's, was he seen,
Nor heard of any other; and the Prince,
His sorrows shaking off, when Kali passed,
After that numbering of the leaves, in joy
Unspeakable, and glowing with new hope,
Mounted the car again, and urged his steeds.
But from that hour the tall Myrobolan,
Possessed by Kali, stood there, sear and dead.

Then onward, onward, speeding like the birds,
Those coursers flew; and fast and faster still
The glad Prince cheered them forward, all elate:
And proudly rode the Raja toward the walls
Of high Vidarbha. Thus did journey down
Exultant Nala, free of trouble now,
Quit of the evil spell, but bearing still
His form misshapen, and the shrunken limb.

AT sunset in Vidarbha (O great King!)
The watchers on the walls proclaimed, "There comes
The Raja Rituparna!" Bhima bade
Open the gates; and thus they entered in,
Making all quarters of the city shake
With rattling of the chariot-wheels. But when
The horses of Prince Nala heard that sound,
For joy they neighed, as when of old their lord
Drew nigh. And Damayanti, in her bower,
Far off that rattling of the chariot heard,
As when at time of rains is heard the voice
Of clouds low thundering; and her bosom thrilled
At echo of that ringing sound. It came
Loud and more loud, like Nala's, when of old,
Gripping the reins, he cheered his mares along.
It seemed like Nala to the Princess then, -
That clatter of the trampling of the hoofs;
It seemed like Nala to the stabled steeds
Upon the palace-roof the peacocks heard
And screamed; the elephants within their stalls

Heard it and trumpeted; the coursers, tied,
Snorted for joy to hear that leaping car;
Peacocks and elephants and cattle stalled
All called and clamored with uplifted heads,
As wild things do at noise of coming rain.

Then to herself the Princess spake: "This car,
The rolling of it, echoing all around,
Gladdens my heart. It must be Nala comes,
My King of men! If I see not, this day,
My Prince that hath the bright and moonlike face,
My hero of unnumbered gifts, my lord,
Ah, I shall die! If this day fall I not
Into his opening arms, - at last, at last,
And feel his close embrace, oh, beyond doubt,
I cannot live! If - ending all - to-day
Nishadha cometh not, with this deep sound
Like far-off thunder, then to-night I'll leap
Into the golden, flickering, fiery dames!
If now, now, now, my lion draws not nigh,
My warrior-love, like the wild elephant,
My Prince of princes, - I shall surely die!
Nought call I now to mind he said or did
That was not rightly said and justly done.
No idle word he spake, even in free speech;
Patient and lordly; generous to bestow
Beyond all givers; scorning to be base,
Yea, even in secret, - such Nishadha was.
Alas! when, day and night, I think of him,
How is my heart consumed, reft of its joy!"

So meditating, like one torn by thoughts,
She mounted to the palace-roof to see
And thence, in the mid-court, the car beheld
Arriving. Rituparn and Vâhuka
She saw, with Vrishni's son, descend and loose
The panting horses, wheeling back the car.

Then Rituparn, alighting, sought the King,
Bhima the Maharaja, far-renowned, -

Whom Bhima with fair courtesies received;
Since well he deemed such breathless visit made
With deep cause, knowing not the women's plots.
"Swâgatam!" cried he; "what hath brought thee, Prince?"
For nothing wist he that the Raja came
Suitor of Damayanti. Questioned so,
This Raja Rituparna, wise and brave,
Seeing no kings nor princes in the court,
Nor noise of the Swayamvara, nor crowd
Of Brahmans gathering, - weighing all those things,
Answered in this wise: "I am come, great Lord,
To make thee salutations!" But the King
Laughed in his heard at Rituparna's word,
That this of many weary yojanas
Should be the mark. "Ahoswid! Hath he passed
Through twenty towns," thought he, "and hither flown
To bid good-morrow? Nay, it is not that.
Good! I shall know it when he bids me know."

Thereat, with friendly speech his noble guest
The King to rest dismissed. "Repose thyself,"
He said; "the road was long; weary thou art.
And Rituparn, with sentences of grace
Replying to this graciousness, was led
by slaves to the allotted sleeping-room
And after Rituparn, Varshneya went.
Vâhuka, left alone, the chariot ran
Into its shed, and from the foamy steeds
Unbuckled all the harness, thong by thong,
Speaking soft words to them; then sat him down,
Alone, forgotten, on the driving-seat.

But Damayanti, seeing Rituparn,
And Vrishni's son, and him called Vâhuka,
Spake sorrowful: "Whose was the thunder, then
Of that fleet car? It seemed like Nala's own
Yet here I see no Nala! Hath yon man
My lord's art learned, or th' other one, that thus
Their car should thunder as when Nala comes?
Could Rituparna drive as Nala doth,

So that those chariot-wheels should sound like his?"
And, after having pondered, (O my King!)
The beauteous Princess sent her handmaiden
To Vâhuka, that she might question him.

"Go, Keshinî," the Princess said; "inquire
Who is that man upon the driving-seat,
Misshapen, with the shrunken arm. Approach
Composedly, question him winningly
With greetings kind, and bid him answer thee
According to the truth. I feel at heart
A doubt - a hope - that this, perchance, may be
My Lord and Prince; there is some new-born joy
Fluttering within my breast. Accost him, girl;
And, ere thou partest, what Parnâda said,
Say thou, and hear him answer, blameless one,
And bring it on thy lips!"

Then went the maid
Demurely, and accosted Vâhuka,
While Damayanti watched them from the roof
"Kushalam tê bravîmi, -health and peace
I wish thee!" said she. "Wilt thou answer true
What Damayanti asks? She sends to ask
Whence set ye forth, and wherefore are ye come
Hither? Vidarbha's Princess fain would know."

"'Twas told my Raja," Vâhuka replied,
That Damayanti for the second turn
Holds her Swayamvara: the Brahman's word
Was, "This shall be to-morrow." So he sped,
Hearing that news, with steeds which in one day
Fly fifty yojanas, swift as the winds,
Exceeding fleet. His charioteer am I."

"Who, then," Keshinî asked, "is he that rode
The third? whence cometh he, and what his race?
And thou thyself whence sprung? and tell me why
Thou servest thus? "

Then Vâhuka replied:
Varshneya is the third who rode with us,
The famous charioteer of Nala he:
When thy Prince fled, he went to Koshala
And took our service. I in horse-taming
And dressing meat have skill; so am I made
King Rituparna's driver and his cook."

"Knoweth Varshneya, then, where Nala fled?
Inquired the maid "and did he tell thee this,
Or what spake he?"

"Of that unhappy Prince
He brought the children hither, and then went
Even where he would, of Nala wotting nought;
Nor wotteth any man, fair damsel! more.
Hidden from mortal eyes Nishadha lives,
Wandering the world, his very body changed.
Of Nala only Nala's own heart knows,
And by no sign doth he bewray himself."

Keshinî said: "That Brahman who did wend
First to Ayodhyâ bore a verse to say
Over and over, everywhere, -strange words,
Wove by a woman's wit. Listen to these:-

Whither art thou departed, cruel lover,
Who stole the half of thy belovèd's cloth,
And left her to awaken, and discover
The wrong thou wroughtest to the love of both?

She, as thou didst command, a sad watch keepth
With woful heart wearing the rended dress.
Prince, hear her cry who thus forever weepeth;
Be mindful, hero; comfort her distress!

What was it thou didst utter, hearing this?
Some gentle speech! Say it again, - the Queen,
My peerless mistress, fain would know from me.
Nay, on thy faith, when thou didst hear that man,

What was it thou repliedst? She would know."

(Descendant of the Kurus!) Nala's heart,
While so the maid spoke, well-nigh burst with grief,
And from his eyes fast flowed the rolling tears;
Put, mastering his anguish, holding down
The passion of his pain, with voice which strove
To speak through sobs, the Prince repeated this:-

"Even against the ruined, rash, ungrateful,
Faithless, fond Prince, from whom the birds did steal
His only cloth, whom now a penance fateful
Dooms to sad days, that dark-eyed will not feel

Anger; for if she saw him she should see
A man consumed with grief and loss and shame
Ill or well lodged, ever in misery,
Her unthroned lord, a slave without a name."

Speaking these verses, woful Nala moaned,
And, overcome by thought, restrained no more
His trickling tears; fast broke they forth (O King!).
But Keshinî, returning, told his words
To Damayanti, and the grief of him.

WHEN Damayanti heard, sore-troubled still,
Yet in her heart supposing him her Prince,
Again she spake: "Go, Keshinî, and watch
Whatever this man doeth; near him stand,
Holding thy peace, and mark the ways of him
And all his acts, going and coming; note
If aught there be of strange in any deed.
Let them not give him fire, my girl, - not though
This hindereth sore; nor water, though he ask
Even with beseeching. Afterward observe,
And bring me what befalls, and every sign
Of earthly or unearthly power he shows;
And whatsoever else Vâhuka doth,
See it, and say."

Thereon Keshinî sped,
Obeying Damayanti, and - at hand -
Whatever by that horse-tamer was wrought,
The damsel watched, and all Ms ways; and came
Back to the Princess, unto whom she told
Each thing Vâhuka did, as it befell,
And what the signs were, and the wondrous works
Of earthly and unearthly gifts in him.

"Subhê!" [1]quoth she, "the man is magical,
But high and holy mannered - never yet
Saw I another such, nor heard of him.
Passing the low door of the inner court,
Where one must stoop, he did not bow his head,
But as he came the lintel lifted up
And gave him space. Bhima the King had sent
Many and diverse meats for Rituparn,
Of beast and bird and fish, - great store of food, -
The which to cleanse some chatties stood hard by,
All empty; yet he did but look on them,
Wishful, and lo! the water brimmed the pots.
Then, having washed the meats, he hastened forth
In quest of fire, and, holding towards the sun
A knot of withered grass, the bright flame blazed

Instant amidst it. Wonderstruck, was I
This miracle to see, and hither ran
With other strangest marvels to impart
For, Princess, when he touched the blazing grass
He was not burned, and water flows for him
At will, or ceases flowing; [2]and this, too,
The strangest thing of all, did I behold, -
He took some faded leaves and flowers up,
And idly handled them; but while his hands
Toyed with them, lo! they blossomed forth again
With lovelier life than ever, and fresh scent,

---

[1] "O Beautiful On,!"
[2] These were some among the special gifts, it will be recalled, given by the gods, after the Swayamvara, to Nala.

Straight on their stalks. These marvels have I seen,
And fly back now to tell thee, mistress dear! "
But when she knew such wonders of the man,
More certainly she deemed those acts and gifts
Betokened Nala; and so minded, full
Of trust to find her lord in Vâhuka,

With happier tears and softening voice she said
To Keshinî: "Speed yet again, my girl -
And, while he wets not, from the kitchen take
Meat he hath dressed, and bring it here to me."
So went the maid, and, waiting secretly,
Brake from the mess a morsel, hot and spiced,
And, bearing it with faithful swiftness, gave
To Damayanti. She (O Kuru King!) -
That knew so well the dishes dressed by him -
Touched, tasted it, and, laughing - weeping - cried,
Beside herself with joy: "Yes, yes; 'tis he
That charioteer is Nala!" Then, a-pant,
Even while she washed her mouth,[1] she bade the maid
Go with the children twain to Vâhuka;
Who, when he saw his little Indrasen

And Indrasena, started up, and ran,
And caught, and folded them upon his breast;
Holding them there, his darlings, each as fair
As children of the gods. Then, quite undone
With love and yearning, loudly sobbed the Prince.

Until, perceiving Keshinî, who watched,
Shamed to be known, he set his children down,
And said: "In sooth, good friend, this lovely pair
So like mine own are, that at seeing them
I am surprised into these foolish tears.
Thou comest here too often; men will think

____

[1] Like a well-bred and pious lady, the utmost emotion does not make Damayanti forget her religious duties. The Law of Manu enjoins (v. 145): "After sleep, after sneezing, eating, drinking, spitting, telling untruths, and before reading the sacred books, let every one, though pure, wash out the mouth."

Thee light, or me; remember, we are here,
Strangers and guests, girl! Go thy ways in peace!"

But seeing that great trouble of his soul,
Lightly came Keshinî, and pictured all
To Damayanti. She, burning to know
If truly this were Nala, bade the girl
Seek the Queen's presence, saying thus for her:
"Mother! long watching Vâhuka, I deem
The charioteer is Nala. One doubt lives, -
His altered form. I must myself have speech
With Vâhuka; thou, therefore, bid him come,
Or suffer me to seek him. Be this done
Forthwith, good mother! - whether known or not
Unto the Maharaja."

When she heard,
The Queen told Bhima what the Princess prayed,
Who gave consent; and having this good leave
From father and from mother, (O my King!)
Command was sent that Vâhuka be brought
Where the court ladies lodged.

So met those twain;
And when Prince Nala's gaze fell on his wife,
He stood with beating heart and tearful eyes.
And when sweet Damayanti looked on him,
She could not speak for anguish of keen joy
To have him close; but sat there, mute and wan,
Wearing a sad-hued cloth, her lustrous hair
Falling unbanded, and the mourning-mark
Stamped in gay ashes on her lovely brow.[1]

And, when she found a voice, these were the words
That came from her: "Didst ever, Vâhuka,-
If Vâhuka thy name be, as thou say'st, -
Know one of noble nature, honorable,

---

[1] I thus understand the Sanskrit word mulapankinî, which Milman unreasonably
reads "mire-defiled."

Who in the wild woods left his wife asleep, -
His innocent, fond wife, -weary and worn?
Know'st thou the man? I'll say his name to thee;
'Twas Nala, Raja Nala! Ah, and when
In any thoughtless hour had I once wrought
The smallest wrong, that he should leave me so,
There in the wood, by slumber overcome?
Before the gods I chose him for my lord,

The gods themselves rejecting; tell me how
This Prince could so abandon, in her need,
His true, his loving wife, she who did bear
His babes, - abandon her to whom he swore
My hand clasped, in the sight of all the gods,
And Agni's self, - 'Thy true lord I will be!'
Thou saidst it! -where is now that promise fled?"

While thus she spake, (O Victor of thy foes!)
Fast from her eyes the woe-sprung waters ran.
And Nala, seeing those night-black,[1] loving eyes
Reddened with weeping, seeing her falling tears;
Brake forth: "Ah! that I lost my throne and realm
In dicing, was not done by fault of mine;
'Twas Kali wrought it; Kali, O my wife,
Drave me to leave thee. Therefore, long ago
That evil one was stricken by the curse
Which thou didst utter, wandering in the wood,

Desolate, night and day, grieving for me.
Possessing me he dwelt; but, cursed by thee,
Tortured he dwelt, consuming with thy words
In fierce and fiercer pain, as when is piled
Brand upon burning brand. But he is gone;
Patience and penance have o'ermastered him.
Princess, the end is redched of our long woes.
That evil one being fled, freeing my will,
See, I am here; and wherefore would I come,
Fairest, except for thee? Yet, answer this:

---

[1] The word is Krishnasar, "essence of blackness."

How should a wife, right-minded to her lord, -
Her own and lawful lord, - compass to choose
Another love, as thou, that tremblest, didst?
Thy messengers over all regions ran,
By the King's name proclaiming: 'Bhima's child
A second husband chooseth for herself,
Whomso she will, - as pleaseth, - being free.'
Those shameless tidings brought the Raja here
At headlong speed - and me!"

Tenderly smiled
Damayanti through her tears, with quivering lips,
And joined palms, answering her aggrievèd Prince
"Judgest thou me guilty of such a sin?
When for thy sake I put the gods aside,
Thee did I choose, Nishadha, my one lord.
In quest of thee did all those Brahmans range
In all ten regions, telling all one tale
Taught them by me; and so Parnâda came
To Koshala, where Rituparna dwells,
And found thee in his house, and spake to thee
Those words, and had thy gentle answer back.
Mine the device was, Prince, to bring thee quick;
For well I wist no man in all this world
Could in one day the fleetest coursers urge
So many yojanas, save thou, dear Prince!
I touch thy feet, and tell thee this in truth
And true it is that never any wrong
Against thee, even in fancy, have I dreamed.
Witness for me, as I am loyal and pure,
The ever-shifting, all-beholding Air,
Who wanders o'er the earth; let him withdraw
My breath and slay me, if I sinned in aught
Witness for me, yon golden Sun who goes
With bright eye over us; let him withhold
Warm life and kill me, if I sinned in aught!
Witness for me the white Moon, whose pale spell
Lies on all flesh and spirit; let that orb
Deny me peace and end me, if I sinned!
These be the watchers and the testifiers,

The three chief gods that rule the three wide worlds;
I cry unto them; let them speak for me;
And thou shall hear them answer for my faith,
Or once again, this day, abandon me."

Then Vayu showed - the all-enfolding Air -
And spake: "Not one wrong hath she wrought thee, Prince,
I tell thee sooth. The treasure of her truth
Faultless and undefilèd she hath kept
By us regarded, and sustained by us,
These many days. Her tender plot it was,
Planned for thy sake, which brought thee - since who else
Could in one day drive threescore vojanas?
Nala, thou hast thy noble wife again;
Thou, Damayanti, hast thy Nala back.
Away with doubting; take her to thy breast,
Thrice happy Prince!"

And while God Vayu spake,
Look! there showered flowers down out of the sky
Upon them; and the drums of heaven ' beat
Beautiful music, and a gentle wind,
Fragrant, propitious, floated, kissing them.
But Nala, when he saw these things befall, -
Wonderful, gracious, -when he heard that voice

Called the great snake to memory: - whereupon
His proper self returned. Bhima's fair child
Divinely sounding (Lord of Bhârat's line
Yielded all doubt of his delightful Love.
Then cast he round about his neck the cloth
Unstained by earth, enchanted -and (O King!)
Saw her dear lord his beauteous form resume.
Ah, Nala! Nala!" cried she, while her arms
Clasped him and clung; and Nala to his heart
Pressed that bright lady, glowing, as of old,
With princely majesty. Their children twain
Next he caressed; while she -at happy peace -
Her beautiful glad face laid on his breast,
Sighing with too much joy. And Nala stood

A great space silent, gazing on her face,
Sorrow-stamped yet, her long, deep-lidded eyes,
Her melting smile, - himself 'twixt joy and woe.

Afterwards, all that story of the Prince,
And all of Damayanti, Bhima's Queen
Told to the Maharaja joyously.
And Bhima said: "To-morrow will I see
When Nala hath his needful offerings made -
Our daughter and this wandering lord well knit."

But all that night they sat, hand clasped in hand,
Rejoicing, and relating what befell
In the wild wood, and of the woful times.
And afterwards, in Bhima's royal house
Serenely dwelled the Princess and the Prince,
Each making for the other peaceful joy.
So in the fourth year Nala was rejoined
To Damayanti, comforted and free,
Restful, attained, tasting delights again.
Also the glad Princess, gaining her lord,
Laid sorrows by, and blossomed forth anew,
As doth the laughing earth when the rain falls,
And brings her unseen, waiting wonders forth
Of blade and flower and fruit. The ache was gone,
The loneliness and load. Heart-full of ease,
Lovelier she grew and brighter, like the moon
Mounting at midnight in the cloudless blue.

THAT night being spent, Prince Nala in his state
Led forth Vidarbha's Pride before the court.
And Bhima - in an hour found fortunate -
Re-wed those married lovers. Dutifully
Nala paid homage to the Maharaj,
And reverently did Damayanti bow
Before her father. He the Prince received
With grace and gladness, as a son restored,
Making fair welcome, and with words of praise
Exalting Damayanti, tried and true;
Which in all dignity Prince Nala took,

Returning, as was meet, words honorable.
Therewith unto the city spread the noise
Of that rejoicing. All the townspeople,
Learning of Nala joyously returned,
Made all their quarters gay with float of flags,
Flutter of cloths, and garlands; sprinkled free
The King's-ways [1] with fresh water, and the cups
Of fragrant flowers; and hung long wreaths of flowers
From door to door the white street-fronts before
And decked each temple-porch, and went about
The altar-gods.

When Rituparna heard
How Vâhuka is Nala in disguise,
And of the meeting, right rejoiced at heart
That Raja grew. And, being softly prayed
By Nala favorable thought, the King
Made royal and gentle answer, with like grace
By Nala met. To whom spake Rituparn:
"Joy go with thee and her, happily joined.
But say, Nishadha, wrought I any jot
Wrongful to thee, whilst sojourning unknown
Within my walls? If any word or deed,
Purposed or purposeless, hath vexed thee, friend,
For one and all thy pardon grant to me!"

And Nala answered: "Never act or word,
The smallest, Raja, lingers to excuse!
If this were otherwise, thy slave was I,
And might not question, but must pardon thee.
Yet good to me thou wert, princely and just,
And kin thou art; and friendly from this time
Deign thou to be. Happily was I lodged,
Well-tended, well-befriended in thy house;
In mine own palace never better stead.
The skill in steeds which pleased thee, that is mine,
And, Raja, I will give it all to thee,
If thou be'st minded."

---

[1] This is the exact Sanskrit word, Râjamârgâ

So Nishadha gave
All his great gift in horses to the King,
Who learned each rule approved, and ordinance;
And, having all this knowledge, gave in turn
His deepest lore of numbers and the dice
To Nala, afterwards departing home
To his own place, another charioteer
Driving his steeds; and, Rituparna gone,
Not long did Nala dwell in Bhima's town.

WHEN one moon he had tarried, taking leave,
Nishadha to his city started forth
With chosen train. A shining car he drove;
And elephants sixteen, and fifty horse,
And footmen thirty score came in the rear.
Swiftly did Nala journey, making earth
Quake 'neath his flying-car; and wrathfully
With quick steps entered he his palace doors.
The son of Virasena, Nala, stood
Once more before that gamester Pushkara!
Spake he: "Play yet again; much wealth is mine,
And that, and all I have, -yea, my Princess, -
Set I for stakes: set thou this realm, and throw
My mind is fixed a second chance to try,
Where, Pushkara, we will play for all or none.
Who wins his throne and treasures from a prince,
Must stand the hazard of the counter-cast,
This is the accepted law. If thou dost blench,
The next game we will play is 'life or death,'
In chariot-fight; when, or of thee or me
One shall lie satisfied: 'Descended realms,
By whatsoever means, are to be sought,'
The sages say, 'by whatsoever, won.'
Choose, therefore, Pushkara, which way of these
Shall please thee; either meet me with the dice,
Or with thy bow confront me in the field."

When Pushkara this heard, lightly he smiled,
Concluding victory sure; and to the Prince

Answered, exulting: "Dishtya![1] hast thou gained
Stakes for a counter-game, Nishadha, now?
Dishtya! shall I have my hard-won prize,
Sweet Damayanti? Dishtya! didst thou come
In kissing-reach again of thy fair wife?
Soon, in thy new gold splendid, she shall shine

Before all men beside me, as in heaven
On Sakra waits the loveliest Apsarâ.[2]
See, now, I thought on thee, I looked for thee,
Ever and ever, Prince. There is no joy
Like casting in the game with such as thee.
And when to-day I win thy blameless one, -
The smooth-limbed Damayanti, - then shall be
What was to be: and I can rest content,
For always in my heart her beauty burns."

Listening the idle talk that babbler poured,
Angry Prince Nala fain had lopped away
His head with vengeful khudga;[3] but, unmoved,
Albeit the wrath blazed in his bloodshot eyes,
He made reply: "Play! mock me not with jests
Thou wilt not jest when I have cast with thee!"

So was the game set, and the Princes threw
Nala and Pushkara, and - the numbers named-

By Nala was the hazard gained: he swept
His brother's stake, gems, treasure, kingdom, off;
At one stroke all that mighty venture won.
Then quoth the conquering Prince to Pushkara,
Scornfully smiling: "Mine is now once more
Nishadha's throne; mine is the realm again,
Its curse plucked forth; Vidarbha's glory thou,
Outcast, shalt ne'er so much as look upon!

---

[1] An exclamation of joy and surprise.
[2] The Apsarâsas are the celestial nyrnphs of Indra's heaven, produced at the churning of the ocean.
[3] A short, broad-bladed sword.

Fool! who to-day becom'st her bond and slave.
Not by thy gifts that evil stroke was wrought
Wherefrom I fled before; 'twas Kali's spell -
Albeit thou knew'st nought, fool - o'ermastered me
Yet will I visit not in wrathful wise
My wrong on thee; Eve as thou wilt; I grant
Wherewith to live, and set apart henceforth
Thy proper goods and substance, and fit food.
Nay, doubt not I shall show thee favor, too,
And be in friendship with thee, if thou wilt,
Who art my brother. Peace abide with thee!"

Thus all-victorious Nala comforted
His brother, and embraced him, sending him
In honor to his town; and Pushkara -
Gently entreated - to Nishadha spake,
With folded palms and humbled face, these words:
"Unending be thy glory. May thy bliss
Last and increase for twice five thousand years,
Who grantest me wherewith to live, just Lord!
And where to dwell." Thereafter, well bested,
Pushkara sojourned with the Prince one moon;
So to his town departed - heart-content -
With slaves and foot-soldiers and followers,
Gay as a rising sun (O Bhârat's glory!)

Thus sent he Pushkara, rich and safe, away.
Then, with flags and drums and jewels, robed and royally arrayed,
Nala into fair Nishadha entry high and dazzling made;
At the gates the Raja, halting, spake his people words of love;
Gathered were they from the city, gathered from the field and grove;
From the mountain and the maidan, all a-thrill with joy to see
Nala come to guard his children. "Happy now our days will be,"
Said the townsfolk, said the elders, said the villagers, "O King!"
Standing all with palms upfolded: "Peace and fortune thou wilt bring
To thy city, to thy country! Boundless welcome do we give,
As the gods in heaven to Indra, when with them he comes to live."

After, when the show was ended, and the city, calm and glad,
Rest from tumult of rejoicing and rich flood of feasting had,

Girt with shining squadrons, Nala fetched his pearl of women home.
Like a queen did Damayanti back unto her palace come,
By the Maharaja Bhima, by that mighty monarch sent
Royally, with countless blessings, to her kindom, in content.
There, beside his peerless Princess, and his children, bore he sway,
Godlike, even as Indra ruling 'mid the bliss of Nandana.[1]
Bore he sway, - my noble Nala, - princeliest of all lords who reign
In the lands of Jambudwipa; [2]winning power and fame again;
Ruling well his realm reconquered, like a just and perfect king,
All the appointed gifts bestowing, all the rites remembering.

---

[1] Nandana is the Paradise of Indra.
[2] Ancient name of India: "The Land of the Rose-apple Tree."

THE ENCHANTED LAKE

THEN Yudhisthira spake to Nakula:
"Thou son of Madri, climb upon a tree,
And look to all ten quarters, if by chance
Water be nigh, or plants which love the pool;
Thy brothers faint with thirst."

So Nakula
Clomb a tall tree; and looking, called aloud:
"Green leaves and water plants I see, which love
The marish and the pool; also I hear
The cry of cranes; yonder will water lie,"

"Go," said the King, "and fetch for us to drink,
Filling thy quiver."

Then sped Nakula,
Obeying Yudhisthira, with swift feet,
And found a crystal pool brimmed to the bank:
The great red-crested cranes stalked on its marge.
And down he flung to drink; but a voice cried:
"Beware to drink, rash youth, ere thou hast made
Answers to such things as I ask of thee
The law of this fair water standeth thus
Arise, and hear, and speak; afterwards drink,
And fill thy quiver!"

But the eager Prince,
Being so parched, quaffed deep, not heeding him,
The Vaksha [1] of the place, and thereupon
Fell lifeless in the reeds.

---

[1] "Yakshas" are supernatural beings of Hindu poetry, resembling our fairies, and called, indeed, punya janas, or "good people." They are very powerful, and generally beautiful in form and benignant.

So, when they looked
To see him coming, and he tarried long,
Again spake Yudhisthira: "Nakula
Lingers too much, my brothers. Sahadev,
Go thou, and bring him back, and bring to drink."

"I go," quoth Sahadev; and sought the pool,
And saw the water, and saw Nakula
Prone on the earth. Then mightily he grieved,
Spying the Prince outstretched , yet, all so fierce
His drouth was, that he ran and flung him down,
Making to quaff; when, once again, the voice

Sounded: "Beware to drink, ere thou dost give
Answer to what things I will ask of thee
This is the law of me, who am the Lord
Of the fair water; rise, and hear, and speak;
Then thou shalt drink and draw."

Yet so the stress
Of thirst o'ercame him, that he heeded not,
But drank, and rose, and - reeled among the reeds
Lifeless.

Then, once again, great Kunti's son
Spake, saying: "O Arjuna, Fear of foes,
These, our twain brethren, tarry; go thyself,
And speed, and bring them back, and bring to drink.
Our trust thou art, for we are sore distressed."

Which hearing, Gudikesá [1] seized his bow
And arrows, and, with drawn sword, sought the pool,
But coming thither, saw those heroes stretched

His brethren, best of men, -in deadly swoon,
Or dead indeed; and deep distraught he stood,
Seeing them thus. All round the wood he gazed,
With lifted bow, and arrow on the string,

____

[1] "He of the knotted locks,"

Seeking some foe; but when none carne in sight,
So wild his thirst was, and the pool so clear,
He bent his knee to drink, but, bending, heard
That voice cry: "Dost thou this without my leave?
Despite me, Kunti's son, thou canst not drink;
And shalt not, till thou makest answer good
Unto my asking; then mayst thou be free,
O born of Bhârata, to drink and draw!"

Thus sternly stayed, the Prince exclaimed in wrath:
Come forth and show thyself, and fight with me
Pierced by my arrows thou shalt yield the pool."
Then shot he shafts this way and that; and spoke
Those spells which make a feathered barb fly straight;
And darts he flung, of magic might, which find
Th' escaping foe, tracking his winding feet;
Karnis, nârâchas, nâlikas [1] he threw, -
That angry Prince, - covering the sky and wood
With searching barbs. Thereat the voice anew
Mocked him, low laughing: "Son of Pritha, vain
Thine anger is; answer me fair, and drink;
But if thou drinkest ere thou answerest,
Thou shalt not live." Yet was his throat so parched
The Prince regarded not, and stooped, and drank,
And fell down dead.

Then Yudhisthira spake:
Bhima, thou Terror of thy foes, see now
Arjuna, Nakula, Sahadev, are gone
To fetch us water, but they come not back.
Seek them, and bring to drink."

And Bhima said,
So be it."And he went unto the place
Where those, his mighty-hearted brethren, lay.

But when he saw them -all three - dead and stark,
Sore mourned that long-armed lord, and gazed around,

---

[1] These are names for different kinds of darts and arrows.

Deeming some Yaksha or some Râkshasa
Had wrought their doom, and chafing for the fight.
"Put first," quoth he, "t'were good to drink," - so sore
The drouth oppressed; and to the pool he sped,
Thinking to quaff, when yet again that voice
Echoed Dare not to drink! So stands the law
Of this fair water; answer first, then drink!"
But Bhima, parched and haughty, answered nought,
Lapping the sweet wave; and in lapping, fell.

Then, long time left alone, Kunti's wise son
Uprose, - great Yudhisthira, - sorrowful,
Perplexed in thought, and strode into the wood:
A leafy depth, where never foot was heard
Of man, but shy deer roamed, and shaggy bears
Rustled, and jungle-hens clucked in the shade;
With tall trees crowded, in whose crown wild bees
Swarmed buzzing, and strange birds builded their nests.
Through this green darkness wending, Yudhisthir
passed to the pool, and marked its silver face
Shine in the light, rimmed round with purple cups
Of lotus- blossoms, all as if 'twere made
By Viswakarnia, architect divine;
And all its gleaming shallows and bright bays
With water-plants were broken, - lilies, reeds;
And framed about with ketuk-groves,[1] and clumps
Of sweet rose-laurel and the sacred fig;
Insomuch that the King stood wondering there,
Albeit heart- sorrowful.

For there he saw,
Stretched dead together, - as the world's lords die,
Indra and all, at every yuga's end, -
His-warrior brethren. Prone Arjuna lay,
Beside his bow and arrow; Bhima prone,
With Nakula and Sahadev; each void
Of life and motion; and, beholding these,

---

[1] The Pandanus odoratissimus.

His soul sank, and he fetched a grievous sigh.
Bitterly at that sight lamented he,
Saying: "Ah, Bhima! O my brother, named
From the grim wolf, I vain is the vow thou mad'st
To break the thigh of fell Duryodhana,
In battle with thy mace. Dead art thou now,
And those words wind. Brother and faithful friend, -
Who wast so princely hearted, and upheld'st
The fortune of the Kurus, - vows of men
Fail ofttimes, being blind, but this of thine
Was noble; wherefore hath it borne not fruit?
O Dhananjaya, conqueror of wealth,
My joy, my brave Arjuna! At thy birth
The glad gods spake to Kunti: 'This thy son
Shall be like Indra with the thousand eyes.'
And northwards of the Paripatra hills
All people cried: 'Here is the chief shall bring
The glory back to us, having such strength

That in the battle none will make him fly,
And none shall stand when he pursueth.' How,
Ah, Jishnu! - how is this betided here,
Killing those hopes with thee, with thee, whose love
Made all our dangers sweet? And Sahadev,
And Nakula, so valiant in the fight,
So high and gallant, gifted like the gods, -
How have ye fallen? Who could conquer you?
Is my heart stone, that now it breaketh not,
Seeing these great twins gone, the first of men,
Heroes, the half of whose renownèd work
Was yet to do? Ye knew the Shastras, -knew
The times and places and observances,
And kept the rites; how lie ye on the earth,
Unconquered ones, thus slain, thus overcome,
And not a wound to show - Day! but the strings
Not slipped into the notches of your bows?"

So broke the sorrow forth from Yudhisthir,
Beholding all four brethren lying still,
Stark, like four corpses set asleep by Death;

Much grieved he, and the marvel chilled his blood:
Nor wist he, though so wise, whither to look
For that which slew them. Yet, close-pondering,
Unto himself he spake: "No hurts they bear
Made by a mortal weapon, nor is print
Of footmark nigh, save theirs; this is some Bhût,
Some spirit of the waste! But let me drink,
And afterward consider; it may be
The vile Duryodhana hath drugged the pool,
By counsel of Gandhâra's King; the wise
Trust never him with senses unsubdued,
To whom things lawful and unlawful count
One and the same; yea, but this thing might be
Wrought by hid hatred of Duryodhana!"

Thus mused the King, but murmured presently:
Pure and unsullied seems the water,- fresh
My brothers' faces are; no poison-stain
Mars limb or lip! 'Tis Yama's self hath come,
The conqueror of all, and slain them here,
Whom none but he dared strike, being so strong."

So saying, to the brink he drew, athirst,
And stooped to drink, when, close at hand, he heard
A bird's cry; and the Yaksha, taking shape,
Spake: "A gray crane I am, feeding on fish
And water-weeds; 'tis I have sent yon four
Into the regions of the dead, and thou
Shalt go, the fifth, great Raja, following them,
Except thou makest answers fair and good
To all which I shall ask. Dare not to drink,
Thou son of Kunti! for my law is strong;
Answer, and afterwards drink thou, and draw."

Spake Yudhisthir: "Who art thou? Art thou chief
Of Rudras, or of Vasus, or Marûts? [1]

---

[1] The Rudras, or "Howlers," eleven in number, and the Marûts, are storm-gods; the eight Vâsus, personifications of natural phenomena, such as water, wind, fire, light, &c.

Tell me! No bird wrought thus, unless a bird
Might overthrow Himavân, and the peaks
Of Paripatra, or the Vindhya crags,
Or Malabar's black ghâts. Ah! terrible
And mighty one, this is a dread deed wrought
This is a marvel, if thou slewedst those
Whom Gods, and Gandharvas, and Asuras,
And Demons dared not face in fight. I know
Nought of thy mind, nor if thou didst this thing
Desiring aught; wonder and fear possess
My burdened heart. I pray thee, show thyself;
Reveal what god thou art who hauntest here."

"Yea, King," came answer, "I am not a bird
Wading the shallows, but a Yaksha dread;
And I, as now thou seest me, killed these four."
Raja (so Vaisampayana, went on),
When Yudhisthira heard those scornful words,
And saw that form, backward he drew a space,
Gazing upon the Shape so fiery-eyed,
Bulked like a crag, with towering head which topped
The fan-palms waving near; shining as shines
The glory of the sun, not to be borne
For splendor; colored like an evening cloud,
And, like a cloud, still shifting. Then it spake,
That monstrous Shade: "These four, though I forbade,
Drank of the pool, despite me, and were slain.
Drink not, O King, if thou desirest life!
O son of Pritha, drink not! Kunti's child,
Answer my questionings; then drink and live!"

"I would not break thy rule," quoth Yudhisthir;
The wise have said, I Keep everywhere the law.'
And, Yaksha, wherein thou wilt question me,
None can speak better than he understands;
So what I know that will I answer. Ask!"

Then thus he questioned, and the King replied.

YAKSHA. What teacheth division 'twixt spirit and frame?
And which is the practice assisteth the same?
What finally freeth the spirit? and how
Doth it find a new being? Resolve me these now.

KING. The Veds division plainly show;
By worship rightly man doth go;
Dharma the soul will surely free;
In truth its final rest shall be.

YAKSHA. How cometh a man in the Veds to be wise?
What bringeth the knowledge of God to his eyes?
What learning shall teach. him the uttermost lore?
And whence will he win it? Reply to these four.

KING. By hearing Scripture man acquires;
By doing it his soul aspires;
The utmost lore is conquiering sense,
Which cometh of obedience.

YAKSHA. How wendeth a Brahman to heavenly rest?
And what is the work which befitteth him best?
And which are the sins that disgrace him? and why
Doth he know himself humble and mortal? Reply!

KING. Reading the Vedas leads to rest;
Pure meditation fits him best;
Slander and cruelty defame;
And Death stamps him and all the same.

YAKSHA. Who is it that, gifted with senses to see,
To hear, taste, smell, handle, and seeming to be
Sagacious, strong, fortunate, able, and fair,
Hath never once lived, though he breatheth the air?

KING. The man who, having, doth not give
Out of his treasure to these five, -
Gods, guests, and Pitris, kin, and friend,
Breathes breath, but lives not to life's end.

YAKSHA. What thing in the world weigheth more than the world?
What thing goeth higher than white clouds are curled?
What thing fleeth quicker than winds o'er the main?
And what groweth thicker than grass on the plain?

KING. A mother's heart outweighs the earth;
A father's fondness goeth forth
Beyond the sky; thought can outpass
The winds; and woes grow more than grass.

YAKSHA. Whose eyes are unclosed, though he slumbers all day?
And what's born alive without motion? and, say,
What moveth, yet lives not? and what, as it goes,
Wastes not, but still waxes? Resolve me now those.

KING. With unclosed eyes a fish doth sleep;
And new-laid eggs their place will keep;
Stones roll - and streams, that seek the sea,
The more they flow the wider be.

VAKSHA. What help is the best help to virtue? and then,
What way is the best way to fame among men?
What road is the best road to heaven? and how
Shall a man live most happy? Resolve me these now.

KING. Capacity doth virtue gain;
Gift-giving, will renown obtain;
Truth is to heaven the best of ways
And a kind heart wins happy days.

VAKSHA. What soul hath a man's which is his, yet another's?
What friend do the gods grant, the best of all others?
What joy in existence is greatest? and how
May poor men be rich and abundant? say thou!

KING. Sons are the second souls of man;
And wives the heaven-sent friends; nor can
Among all joys health be surpassed
Contentment answereth thy last.

YAKSHA. Which virtue of virtues is first? and which bears
Most fruit? and which causeth the ceasing of tears?

KING. To bear no malice is the best;
And reverence is fruitfullest;
Subduing self sets grief at rest.

YAKSHA. Still tell me what foeman is worst to subdue?
And what is the sickness lasts lifetime all through?
Of men that are upright say which is the best?
And of those that are wicked, who passeth the rest?
KING. Anger is man's unconquered foe;
The ache of greed doth never go
Who loveth most of saints is first
Of bad men cruel men are worst.

YAKSHA. Good Prince, tell me true, is a Brahmana made
By birthright? or shall it be rightfully said,
If he reads all the Veds, and the Srutis doth know,
He is this? or doth conduct of life make him so?

KING. O Yaksha, listen to the truth:
Not if a man do dwell from youth
Beneath a Brahman's roof, nor when
The Srutis known to holy men
Are learned, and read the Vedas through,
Doth this make any Brahman true.
Conduct alone that name can give
A Brahmana must steadfast live,
Devoid of sin, and free from wrong;
For he who walks low paths along,
Still keeping to the way, shall come
Sooner and safer to his home
Than the proud wanderer on the hill;
And reading, learning, praying, still
Are outward deeds which ofttimes leave
Barren of fruit minds that believe.
Who practises what good he knows,
Himself a Brahmana he shows;
And if an evil nature knew

The sacred Vedas through and through,
With all the Srutis, still must he,
Lower than honest Sudra [1] be.
To know and do the right, and pay
The sacrifice, in peace alway:
This maketh one a Brahmana.

YAKSHA. Right skilfully hast thou my questionings mut
Most pious of princes, and learned I but yet
Resolve me, who liveth though death him befall?
And what man is richest and greatest of all?

KING. Dead though he be, that mortal lives
Whose virtuous memory survives;
And richest, greatest, that one is
Whose soul -indifferent to bliss

Or misery, to joy or pain,
To past or future, loss or gain
Sees with calm eyes all fates befall,
And, needing nought, possesseth all.

Then spake the Yaksha: "Wondrously, O King,
Hast thou replied, and wisely hast fulfilled
The law of this fair water: therefore, drink,
And choose which one of these thy brethren dead
Shall live again."

So Yudhisthira said:
Let Nakula, O Yaksha, have his life,
My dark-browed brother with the fiery eyes,
Straight like a sâla-tree , broad-chested, tall,
That long-armed lord."

"But see where Bhima lies
Dead," spake the spirit, "dearest unto thee;
And where Arjuna sleeps, thy guard and guide.
Why dost thou crave the life of Nakula -

____

[1] The name of the lowest caste.

Not thine own mother's son - in Bhima's stead,
Who had the might of countless elephants,
Whom all the people called thy 'Well-Beloved'?
Or wouldst thou see Nakula alive again
In place of great Arjuna, thine own blood.,
Whose valor was the tower of Pandavas?"

But Yudhisthira answered: "Faith and Right,
Being preserved, save all, and, being lost,
Leave nought to save: these therefore I will set
First in my heart. Faithful and right it is
To choose by justice, putting self aside.
Let Nakula live, O Yaksha, for men call
King Yudhisthira "just"; nor will he lose,
Even for love, that name; make Nakula live
Kund and Madri were my father's wives;
Shall one be childless, and the other see
Her sons returning? Madri is to me
As Kunti, as my mother, at this hour;
As she who bore me she that bore the twins;
And justice shall she have, since I am judge.
Let Nakula live, thou Yaksha!"

Then the voice
Sighed sweet, evanishing Ah, noblest Prince,
Ah, Best of Bhârat's Ene I as thou art just,
Lo! all thy brethren here shall. live again."

THE SAINT'S TEMPTATION.[1]

BORN of the White Doe, in the woods he dwelt,
That sinless saint, pious and mild and pure,
Sad-minded, solitary; for his eyes
Had never lighted on a human face,
Except his sire, Vibhandika's; and thus
Always young Rishyasringa's heart was set
On sanctities (O King!).

At which far time
Lômapâd, friend of Dasarath, was Lord
In Anga. He, 'tis told, spake falsely once
Unto a Brahmana; and thereupon
The Brahmans fled from that dishonored court.
So, when no priest was left, no purôhit,
He, of the thousand eyes, Indra, withheld
His rains, whereby sore suffered all the folk:
And (O my King!) Lômapâd sent in grief,
Praying his wisest if they knew the cause
Of Indra's wrath, and what should make him rain.

Thus questioned, these took counsel; and one spake,
A chief of sages, - "O superior Lord,
The Brahmanas are angered for thy word
Forsworn: thou therefore make them fit amends;
And hither bring Rishyasring, who dwells
Alone, amid the groves, holy and mild;
Whose eyes have never seen a woman's face;
Whose heart is pure. If the fair boy shall come,
The clouds of Indra will let fall their drops
That very day; of this thing doubt ye not!"

---

[1] A curious interest attaches to this legend, now for the first time extracted from the Mahâbhârata. It is familiar in Ceylon as the Nâlini Jâtaka, Buddha being made the sage Vibbandika, and the princess Nâlini-daughter of the Raja of Benares-the temptress of the youthful saint.

Hearing their words, the Raja purged his guilt
With princely gifts, soothing the Brahmanas;
And when their hearts were good, he came again
Unto his kingdom, making all folks glad.
And, next, the Lord of Anga called his best
Among the ministers to compass means
How Rishyasringa. might be brought; and those,
Deep read in Shastra, Artha, Niti, all, -
Counselled the wiles of woman; whereupon
A band of comely, winsome girls were bid
Unto the palace, skilled in arts to please.
And the King, said: "Beautiful damsels, bring
Rishyasringa hither, that saint's son;
Entice, allure, persuade, - ye know men's hearts."
But they, fearing the King, yet fearing more
The saint's curse, if they vexed him, one by one
Answered: "Yea, Raja, hearts of men we know;
But in this thing how shall we serve thy will?"

Then one arose, white-haired and wrinkled deep,
An ancient dame, who spake unto the King:
"See, Maharaja! I will fetch this boy,
Albeit an ocean of austerities.
Do thou command that there be granted me
Means for my need, that so I may prevail,
And bring the Rishi's son, this pearl of saints."

"What needest thou?" quoth he. And when he knew,
Much store of silver and of gold and gems
He gave the dame; who from the ring of girls,
Laughing, drew forth the fairest, wilfullest;
And muttering, "He will come!" passed to the woods.

And there she built - (so Lomarsha went on)
Not by the King's word, but her own device,
A floating bower to swim upon the stream.
Full sweet she fashioned it, from woven boughs
Of verdure, interlaced with palms and vines,
And clasped by climbing stems, and hung with fruit

Golden and rosy, and with bright blooms decked;
Afterwards, on the river launched her boat, --
The damsel seated 'neath its leafy screen, -
So that it came, with paddle, stream, and breeze,
Through the trees stealing, down the silvery road
Softly and silent to the Rishi's haunt;
When lightly tripped the lovely girl ashore,
And, looking in his eyes, demurely spake: -

"O Muni! [1] is it peace with you? are all the Rishis well?
And have you roots and fruits enough? and take you joy to dwell
All lonely in this hermitage, which I am come to see?
And add you, day by day, dear saint, unto your sanctity?
And, Brahman, doth your sire rejoice to watch you fast and pray?
And do you read, O Rishyasring! the Vedas every day?"

Answered that blushing boy delightedly:

O unknown one, who shinest like the splendor of a star,
Peace and good will! for due to thee my salutations are
Accept, I pray thee, at my hands, the Padya [2] and this thrift
Of roots and fruits, as duty bids, a hermit's humble gift;
And be thou pleased upon this mat of kusa grass to sit,
Or, better, let the black deer's skin be smoothly spread on it.
Fair is the day which bringeth thee; O sweet saint, where may be
Thy hermitage, and what vow fills the holy hours of thee?

Right archly answered him the laughing girl: -

"O son of pious Kasyapa, my charming bower lies
Under a mountain far removed from these austerities,
Three yojanas away, - away, - nor is it meet for me

Thus to be reverenced, nor to touch this water, nor to see
A Rishi kneeling at my feet; far otherwise my state!
Love is the vow which fills my life, and makes my heart elate."

---

[1] This word signifies "saint," as also Rishi.
[2] It was the graceful and wholesome custom of Indian hospitality to offer water for washing the feet (padya) to a stranger or guest arriving from a journey.

Perplexed, yet radiant, the boy replied:
What should I do to pleasure thee? I 'll bring thee fruits we find
Within our groves, bhallatakas, ingudas with gold rind;
Karushakas, amâlakas, dhanwanas honey-sweet,
Or pippalas; see, these are here; wilt thou not take and eat?"

But smilingly she put them by, and reached
Rare cakes to him, spiced as no hermit knows,
Pleasant of taste, which the boy ate with joy.
And on his neck and wrists lightly she strung
Garlands of subtle-scented flowers; and crowned
Her own bright brows; and drew a light robe on,
Laughing; and so, with murmuring song, unbound
Her body-cloth, and, waving, weaving it,
Paced the soft Kanduka,[1] with beating feet
And bosoms lithely swayed, as flower-cups sway
When the wind shakes their clusters; - at the last
Danced to his side, and for a moment set
Palm to his palm and limb to limb, and lip
To trembling lip, and breast to beating breast:
Then turned aside, and drew the branches down
Of sarja, tilah, and asoka trees,
Plucking their buds, shameless and well-content
Because she saw love lighted in his heart.
For, knowing well her triumph, and the saint
Obtained, once more she clasped her soft brown arms
About him, and with eyes fixed on his eyes
Withdrew; having enkindled passion's flame
Where only fires of sacrifice had burned.

WHEN she was gone, young Rishyasringa stood
As one some dream of heaven hath left distraught,
Spiritless - then within his lonely cell
Sit, with lace fixed through many silent hours,
Her beauties meditating.

Presently

---

[1] A kind of dance in which the performer plays with a ball as she dances.

Vibhandaka, of Kasyapa the son,
Returned. Much insight of the Veds had bleared
His ancient orbs; a thick pile covered him,
Body and legs and arms, to the finger-ends;
A holy man; purified, dedicate
To contemplation. He, arriving, saw
The lad in deep thought plunged, sitting apart
Dejected, fetching sigh on sigh, with glance
Upturned. Whereat inquired Vibhandaka:
My child, why hast thou gathered not the wood?
Didst thou perform the sacrifice to-day?
And didst thou lead the calf to suck the cow?[1]

Why art thou sad? I pray thee tell me true, -
Hath one been with thee here to-day? "

The boy
Gave answer: "Yea, a Brahmacharya came.
His[2] locks were braided, and his comely form
Seemed nor too tall nor short; fair-voiced he was,
Colored as is new gold, with broad bright eyes
Which were like lotus-blossoms. As gods shine,
So - of his own divine grace - glittered he
A glory had he like the sacred sun;
And, ah! his dark, deep glance; and oh, his hair
Tied tip with blue; sweet-smelling, lustrous, long!
A necklace curled and clung about his neck,
Sparkling like lightning on a dusky sky;
And underneath his throat swelled forth to sight
Two globes, flower-soft and smooth, fair-fashioned, large.
His waist so tapered back and front came close; [3]

Below, his hips outrounded wondrously;
A jewelled girdle hung above his thighs,
And some strange tinkling ornaments adorned

---

[1] This was the sacred cow, kept at the hermitage for religious uses.
[2] Rishyasringa takes his visitant for a man, knowing no better.
[3] This is a literal transcript from the Sanskrit, which means that the waist was so
small (a great charm with Indian poets) as to be almost imperceptible.

His feet. Also, upon his arms were gems
Which chattered like the breast-beads of my string,
(Ah, but so musically!) when he moved, -
'Twas as the songs of wild swans on our lake.
The cloths he wore showed goodly, -not like mine.
And when he spoke, those honeyed words which fell
Gladdened my heart and passed into my soul,
Deep -deep, till dearer seemed it than the notes
Of Koils piping! Also, as the woods-
When in the Madhva month the breezes blow -
Shake fragrance forth, so there did waft from him
Sweet breaths on every air. Over his brows
The locks sat smooth, drawn forward from his braids;
And in his ears swung little painted stones
Brighter than chakravâka birds. Sometimes
With skilful hand he tossed a ball aloft,
Which fell to earth, and, bounding to his palm,
Was beaten back again, and yet again,
Wondrous to see; while this and that way waved
His body like a tree which the wind bends.
Ah, while I saw him so, like a young god,
My heart grew full. I worshipped that fair saint.
Full oft, too, he embraced me ' holding me
Close, by the hair, and, drawing down my cheek,
And covering up my mouth with his soft mouth,
Upon my lips made tender sounds,- and this
Gave me strange joy! He would not willingly
Accept 'foot-water,' nor the fruits I brought.
He had a vow was otherwise, he said;
But showed me unknown fruits, more delicate
Than aught we ever taste of here; no rind
They had, nor flesh like ours. Also he gave
Sweet juices to me, which I drank, and felt
A quickening glow, lifting my eyebrows up.
Those wreaths of scented blossoms, strung with silk,
Are from his hand; he left them here, dear saint
(Who by his fasts, no doubt, so splendid shows,)
When he withdrew to seek his hermitage.
Now he is gone, I am become as nought;
My senses fail, my body burns. I ask

Only to go to him, or else that he
Should always come to us. Father, demand
His presence; learn his Brahmacharya's name.
I wish to exercise with that wise man
The penance they perform; I long to do it;
My heart will break, if I see him no more!"

Vibhandaka spake sternly: "Son, there walk
Wonderful Rakshasîs in this our wood,
Dreadful for strength and cunning comeliness;
Ofttimes to interrupt our rites they seek;
Ofttimes, with winsome wiles, and beauteous shapes,
Tempt saints to abandon Swarga's heavenly rest.
He who will rule his mind and reach toward bliss,
With such makes no society, nor looks
The way of those, th' abominable, who snare
The pious. Yea, my son, the foods she gave
Are evil and forbidden, and conduce
To sin. Yon wreaths, moreover, must not lie
Within a hermitage, where Munis live;
For soul- corrupting is their subtle scent.
Nay, 'twas a Rakshasî!"

So did the sage
Counsel that youthful saint, admonishing him,
And afterwards set forth to seek the witch;
But nowhere finding her, came home again.

Yet it befell, upon another day
Vibliandaka went forth to pluck those fruits
Which are most meet to make the sacrifice
Of Sravan; and she came again, the girl,
Silently shining through the trees; and he
Saw her, and seeing, utterly forgot
Rishis and Rakshasîs, so joyed he was,
So with strong love transported; for she sighed,
"Rishyasring!" And with one word he took
Her palm, and led her to the lonely hut,
Whose porch they entered.

Afterwards (O King!)
Langhingly did she win him to the bank
With honeyed arts, and lightly him entranced,
Floating and fondling down the silvery stream,
Until they came to Anga. There she drew
The green boat in, and moored it 'neath the shade
Love's ark, - plain to be seen, and by all folk
Named Navyasrama, "The Floating Shrine."
So Lômapâd brought in the Rishi's son:
And lo! great Indra's wrath was gone; the rain
Burst o'er the land, and drenched the thirsty fields
But Rishyasringa to his forest-cell
Came back no more!

THE BIRTH OF DEATH

I.

I will relate
An ancient story for thy comfort, Prince,
By Narad told to King Akampana:
For that great lord had lost his only son,
Which is of earthly woes hardest to bear.
Tliou, too, shalt learn how Death began, and this
Shall free thee from the ache of love bereaved.
Hear the old story; it is sweet to hear, -
Excellent, holy, purging sins away,
Prolonging life because it stayeth grief,
Good for the heart and soul, strengthening the will
Best of auspicious scriptures. Nay, I say,
To tell or hear this rede is all as if
The blessed Veds were chanted; it should be
Said with the morning prayer for kings to con,
If they will keep their children, realms, and wealth
With minds at ease.

My son, in ages past,
In the far Krita Yuga, lived this King
Akampana. His foes beset him sore,
And slew in fight Hari, his son, a prince,
God Narayen's match for might, youthful and fair,
Skilful in arms, wise, pleasant, in the war
Fearless as Sákra. But they hemmed him round,
Striking such blows amidst his enemies,
That when he fell there lay about his corpse
A bloody belt of chiefs and elephants.

Long mourned the King, his sire, by night and day
Weeping, knowing no joys, uncomforted;
Whom that most holy saint, great Narada,

Hearing his grief, in pity visited.
But when the King saw Narad entering,
Uprose he from the dust, and clasped those feet,
And poured his sorrows into those wise ears;
Recounting all the battle, how 'twas lost,
And how the Prince fell! "Ah, my brave, fair son
So brake he forth, - "Oh, my most gallant boy!
That wast upon our side like Indra's self
For help; like Vishnu, in thy shining mail, -
Slain art thou 'midst thy foes. Ah, Bhagavan!
Ah, Rishi! he is gone; my pride is dead!
What is this Death? Whence cometh it? What curse
Hath given it means and might and power to kill,
Blasting the bloom of life? Thou, who art wise,
Tell me the truth of this; I crave to know."

Then Narad, hearing his most piteous cry,
That teacher of the truth, spake tenderly
The ancient tale I tell, which whoso hears
Ile shall not weep though his one son be dead.

Narada said; "Listen, thou long-armed King,
And grieve no more when thou hast heard. At first,
Far back, in the beginning, He who rules,
Almighty shining Bhrahma, made what lives
To live unchanged; so was there length of days
Illimitable, but not growth in days,
Which comes of change; and Brahma, seeing His worlds
Fixed in fair changelessness, waxed ill content,
Bethinking to unmake what He had made,
That good should pass to better and there went,
O Monarch! from the discontent of Him
Bethinking how He should destroy to save
A flame, the spirit of His brooding thought,
Which, filling all the regions, had consumed
The heavens and earth and worlds from west to east
From north to south, the heavens and earth and worlds,
With all their creatures,- those which live and move,
And those which live unmoving, plants and trees.
So was that thought of Brahma terrible.

"But, thereupon, he of the matted locks,
Hara,-whom men do also Sthánu call,
King of night-wandering ghosts, Shiva the god, -
Unto dread Brahma's presence straight repaired.
Awful in sunlike majesty sat He;
And, seeing Hara at His feet, come there
For love of living beings: 'Son!' He said,
'What need hath brought thee? Let the wish be known;
That which thou dost desire, it shall be wrought;
For thou art Sthánu, and thy will is mine.'

"Spake Hara: 'O Thou Light of all the worlds!
Thine are the worlds, and Thou hast peopled them;
And all things in their orders are by Thee,
And in Thee live. Wilt Thou not save Thine own?
But now they fear to perish everywhere,
Slain by this fire which flameth from Thy mood;
And I, who see it, and who love them, come,
Moved with compassion. Have Thou mercy, Lord!'

"Brahma replied: 'I did not think to slay.
Lo! I am favorable. Life shall live;
For love, not hate, this mood did move in Me;
Because the angel of the earth hath come,
Constantly praying, "Father, lighten me;
Make and unmake this burden sore to bear,
My children, lest we multiply to harm."
Yet, having made them, how should I unmake,
Seeing I gave gifts indestructible,
Giving their lives? I cannot slay, yet these
Must change; therefore that mood did move in Me.'

"Spake Hara: 'O Protector of the worlds
Be favorable still, be wroth no morc;
Let not these lives, moving and motionless,
Perish, O Bhagavan! Let there be henceforth
Three states of time for children of the earth, -
The past, the present, and the future - these
Let them possess, Thou Lord of all! Thy mind

Burneth in moving, and therewith a flame
Proceeded, scorching mountains, rivers, lakes,
Forests, and beasts that dwell there, and the beings,
Moving and motionless, of all the earth.
Ah, Bhagavan, be Thou then propitious; yield
Thine ill-content which slayeth. This I crave.
Also the flame, which hath proceeded forth
By reason of it, draw it back, dread Lord,
Into Thyself - from Thee it sprang. Thou art
Master, to bless or ban. Make Thine acts bless
These that are Thine, to sweep away or save
These that must perish if Thou pity not.
O Maker who unmakest! I am here-
The messenger of ill the guardian gods
Which keep Thy worlds - beseeching Thee, Supreme,
Destroy not that which Thou hast wrought so fair
For this, at Thy great feet I bend and plead.'

"Hearing Maliddev's prayer," quoth Narada,
The awful Brahma gave consent, and drew
Back to Himself that earth-devouring flame.
Then He who maketh and unmaketh worlds
Spake of the making and unmaking, -how
The purpose groweth so. And when the fire
Was wholly quenched, and all His spirit still,
Lo! Brahma meditated; and there rose,
Live from His thought, a presence feminine,
Delicate, tender, splendid, with great eyes.
Dark the sweet face was, dark the stately limbs
But beauty blossomed red on lip and breasts,
And in her ears swung ear-rings of soft gold.
She, being so born, drew backward from the throne,
Awe-struck to gaze upon those gods. But He
Who maketh and unmaketh, spake to her,
Saying: 'Thou Death, thou Mrityu, go, destroy
Those that must die. I have created thee
Unto this work; bring to appointed end
The moving and unmoving; kill and slay
All creatures at their time. This is My will:
Obey and fear not.'

"Thus commanded, Death-
Fair Mrityu, with those eyes like lotuses-
Spake not, but bowed her head and sobbed; her tears
Fast welling; so that on dread Brahma's hand
Fell the bright tears, - for Brahma drew her close,
Saying: 'I bid thee for the good of all.'"

II.

Bur Narada went on. "Then she assuaged
Her sorrow, and replied: 'Father and Lord!'-
Clasping her palms across her beauteous breast,
And trembling like a tendril in the wind, -
'Father and Lord!' sighed Mrityu, 'wherefore, then,
Mad'st Thou me woman? How shall I fulfil
This drcadful duty, this injurious task?
I shall be guilty, I shall be defiled.
Be gracious; let this work light not on me
Why must they die? The friend, the citizen,
The son, the mother, father, brother, bride,
And bridegroom, - all so happy, all so fair, -
Why should these be destroyed? I am afraid
To kill them; I shall sadden at their tears,
Grieve with their groans. Master of all! dear God
Bid me not dwell with Yama, slaying men.
I pray Thee rather give me leave to live
In holy silences and pains and prayers.
This boon I crave, great Father! grant the boon;
And I, Thy child, will go to Dhenuka,
Where I will dwell in sacred solitudes,
Religious, worshipping Thee. But, God of gods,
I shall not have the heart to take away
The dear lives of the dying creatures. Save,
Save me from such a sin!'

"Brahma replied:
Mrityu, thou art created unto this,
To make an end of all that lives. Go, child;
Make them to end, each at his time; spare none:

Such is My will, and never otherwise;
Thou shalt be blameless doing Brahma's will.'

"But she," thus Narada went on, "stood there,
To slay reluctant, clasping pitying palms
Across her breast, and lifting eyes of ruth
To Brahma's eyes. Thereat there spread in heaven
Silence a space, whilst Death, for love of men,
Gazed on the face of God, and that dread face
Waxed well contented - and great Brahma smiled,
Looking upon His creatures, who therewith
Fared well throughout the three wide worlds, because
The countenance of Him was glad again.

"So passed she from the Almighty Presence, mute,
This tender angel, sent to slay mankind,
Refusing still to slay; and forthwith went
To Dhenuka, where, countless ages through,
In meditation and rapt vows she stood
Fixed like a rock:[1] - all for the love of men,
For sixteen padmas -[2] stood she, seeking grace,
Withholding heart and soul from peace and joy;
And afterward, for padmas twenty-five,
Praying for men; and then through many, more
She sojourned with the creatures of the field,
Praying for them. Next, upon Nanda's banks,-
Nanda which flows cool, holy, crystal-pure,-
Seven thousand years and one kept she firm fast
And afterward went east to Kausikî,
Where dews and airs of heaven were all her food
Until, accomplishing the pilgrimage,
By Panchaganga, and at Ganga's wave
Under the feet of sacred Himalay,
And so to topmost Himalay, where gods
Have offered sacrifice, she, too, a god, -
Lay prostrate, praying, still as is a stone.
And yet again at Naimish, Pushkara,

---

[1] The Sanskrit phrase signifies "standing on one leg."
[2] A padma is a thousand billion years.

Gokarna, and Malaya - wheresoe'er
The holiest places are - there sojourned she,
Fasting and meditating, making vows
For men to Brahma, suing Him for them.

"Whereby the Eternal Father of the worlds,
Being well pleased," quoth Narad, "called to her
With kindly mind, saying: 'My Mrityu!
Why dost thou exercise such heavy vows?'

"And gentle Death answered the Lord of life
'That I may never have, O Lord! to kill
Thy creatures, and that they may dwell in peace
This thing I ever wish, this boon I crave.
Master and Father! I did fear the guilt
Of slaying, and I feared to disobey;
Therefore I make these penances, Supreme
Comfort me, who am Thine, and terrified;
Forgive me, for I would be innocent;
Have pity, Lord of lords! on me and these.'

"Then He that knows what was, is, and will be,
Made mild reply: 'Blood-guilty art thou not,
O Mrityu! if thou slayest these which live.
What I have uttered, I have uttered. Vain
Can never be My words. These are to die.
Go, gentle spirit! therefore, slay Me these
Slay all four orders of the things which live
Thee shall the Eternal Virtue purify;
Thee shall the mighty ones who guard My worlds
Succor and aid. Yama shall help thee; plagues,
Pestilence, death, shall be thy ministers;
And I, the Almighty God, before all gods,
Give thee this sign, that, being free from sin,
Thou shalt be called "Passionless" Nirajis,
She that doth slay for love, and, slaying, saves.'

"So once again, commanded past reply,
Mrityu her meek palms folded o'er her breast,

And bowed her brow, and answered: 'If, dread Lord!
This must be done, and I must be the means,
Upon my head be put Thy dread behest
Yet let it be Thy will I strike them not:
Let their sins slay them, and die so with them.
Avarice, ambitions, envies, calumnies,
Wars, wraths, hates, conquests, follies, passions, plots
Of mutual mischiefs, - let those work Thy word,
And bring to end the beings suffering them.'

"'Thus it shall be,' spake Brahma. 'Go, fair child!
Fulfil My purpose, make death enter so;
Thou shalt be blameless now and evermore.
See! the bright tears that fell upon My hand
From forth thine eyes I turn to woes of flesh,
Which shall consume them, -aches, diseases, griefs,
Born of thy sorrow these will smite; but, born
Of thy compassion, these shall heal with peace
When the day cometh that each one must die.
Fear not! thou shalt be innocent; thou art
The solace, as the terror, of all flesh,
Righteous and rightful, doing Brahma's will.
Therefore fare forth and slay, making these end
With pangs of passion, sting's of wild desires,
Vain sins which kill. This shall thy virtue be
And thou shalt purify thee by thyself,
Making the good wax and the evil wane
By nature of the evil's self, - by wrongs,
By wrath, by lust, self-love, and sinfulness.'

"So, ever since that time," quoth Naxada,
Mrityu, no longer thinking to resist,
Works the great will of God, and slays what lives,
Taking the breath of creatures at life's close;
Not with her own kind hand; she doth not kill!
By ills and pests and hurts which evil breeds-
As many as those tender tears that rolled
From forth her eyes -they perish; so men call

Their plagues Vyâdhi, that which 'hunts' [1] to death,

"Wherefore, my King said Narad, "it is vain
To mourn the dead. The elements divine,
Which enter in at birth, come forth at death.
All changes; and the gods are mortal, too.
But thou lament no more thy princely son;
He hath attained that excellent abode,
Airy, invisible, which knows not time,
Nor chance, nor any change. Weep not for him!
He sits with kings and heroes who are passed
Into the everlasting, happy home,
Where no wars are, nor wounds, and good men dwell.

"King! this is death! this is that Mrityu!
Thus, when the hour is come, the creatures end,
Obeying the vast purposes of Him
Who maketh and unmaketh. Mrityu takes
Their breath. She slays not; of themselves they die
The gentle spirit with the staff in hand [2]

Strikes none, but pities all. Therefore the wise,
Knowing that such is Brahma's will and good,
Never lament their dead; grieve thou no more."

AND when the holy Narada made end
(Vyâsa said), this King Akampana
Shcd no more tears, but spake unto the saint:
"Lo! now my woe is gone, my heart is healed!
O wisest of all Rishis, I have peace;
I thank thee for the blessing of such lore
I clasp thy feet." Therewith Narada went
To Nandana, leaving him comforted.
Son of the Pandavas, be patient, too!
Thy Prince, thy gallant Abhimanyu,
Fell like a lord of men, and hath his meed

---

[1] There is a play here upon the two Sanskrit words, vâdhi, "sickness," and vyâdha, "a hunter."
[2] The Sanskrit epithet is Dandapani.

In Swarga with the blessed. Rise thou up,
Quit grief, and take thy weapons, and renew
The battle with thy brothers on the plain.

Whoso reads and whoso hears
This fair story of old years,
Well and wisely gives his pains;
Since thereby his spirit gains
Piety and peace and bliss;
Nay, and heavenward leadeth this;
And, on earth, its wisdom brings
Wealth and health and happy things

THE NIGHT OF SLAUGHTER

To Narayen, Best of lords, be glory given,
To great Saraswati, the Queen in heaven;
Unto Vyâsa, too, be paid his meed,
So shall this story worthily proceed.

"THOSE vanquished warriors then," Sanjaya said,
Fled southwards and, near sunset, past the tents
Unyoked; abiding close, in fear and rage.
There was a wood beyond the camp, untrod,
Quiet; and in its leafy harbor lay
The Princes, some among them bleeding still
From spear and arrow gashes; all sore spent,
Fetching faint breath, and fighting o'er again
In thought that battle. But there came a noise
Of Pandavas pursuing, -fierce and loud
Outcries of victory; whereat these chiefs
Sullenly rose, and yoked their steeds again,
Driving due east; and eastward still they drave
Under the dusk, till drouth and desperate toil
Stayed horse and man; then took they lair again
The panting horses, and the Princes, wroth
With chilled wounds, and the death-stroke of their King.

.   .   .   .   .

Now were they come, my Prince! Sanjaya said,
Unto a jungle thick with stems, whereon
The tangled creepers coiled; here entered they,
Watering the horses at a stream, and pushed
Deep in the thicket. Many a beast and bird
Sprang startled at their feet; the long grass stirred
With serpents creeping off - the woodland flowers
Shook, where the pea-fowls hid; and, where frogs plungèd,
The swarm rocked all its reeds and lotus-buds.

A banian-tree, with countless dropping boughs
Earth-rooted, spied they, and beneath its aisles
A pool; hereby they stayed, tethering their steeds,
And, dipping water, made the evening prayer.

"But when the 'Daymaker' sank in the west,
And Night descended,- gentle, soothing Night,
Who comforts all, with silver splendor decked
Of stars and constellations, and soft folds
Of tender darkness drawn,- then the wild things
Which roam in darkness woke, wandering afoot
Under the gloom. Horrid the forest grew
With roar and yelp and yell, around that place
Where Kripa, Kritavarman, and the son
Of Drona lay beneath the banian-tree,
Full many a piteous passage instancing
In their lost battle-day of dreadful blood;
Till sleep fell heavy on the wearied lids
Of Bhoja's child and Kripa. Then these lords,
To princely life and silken couches used,
Sought on the bare earth slumber, spent and sad,
As homeless outcasts lodge.

"But, O my King!
There came no sleep to Drona's angry son,
Great Aswatthâman. As a snake lies coiled
And hisses breathing, so his panting breath
Hissed rage and hatred round him, where he lay,
Chin uppermost, arm-pillowed, with fierce eyes
Roving the wood, and seeing sightlessly.
Thus chanced it that his wandering glances turned
Into the fig-tree's shadows, where there perched
A thousand crows, thick roosting, on its limbs, -
Some nested, some on branchlets, - deep asleep,
Heads under wings, all fearless; nor, O Prince!
Had Aswatthâman more than marked the birds,
When fierce there fell out of the velvet night,
Silent and terrible, an eagle-owl,
With wide, soft, deadly, dusky wings, and eyes
Flame-colored, and long claws, and dreadful beak,

Like a winged sprite, or great Garood himself.
Offspring of Bhârata! it lighted there
Upon the banian bough; hooted - but low -
The fury smothering in its throat, then fell
With murderous beak and claws upon those crows;
Rending the wings from this, the legs from that,
From some the heads, of some ripping the crops;
Till, tens and scores, the fowl rained down to earth
Bloody and plucked, and all the ground waxed black
With piled crow-carcasses; whilst that great owl
Hooted for joy of vengeance, and again
Spread the wide, deadly, dusky wings.

"Up sprang
The son of Drona: 'Lo! this owl,' quoth he,
'Teacheth me wisdom - lo! one slayeth so
Insolent foes asleep. The Kuru Lords
Are all too strong in arms by day to kill;
They triumph, being many. Yet I swore
Before the King, my father, I would kill
And kill, -even as a foolish fly should swear
To quench a flame. It scorched; and I shall die
If I dare open battle - but by art
Men vanquish fortune and the mightiest odds.
If there be two ways to a wise man's wish,
But only one way sure, he taketh that
And if it be an evil way, condemned
For Brahmans, yct the Kshattriya may do that
Which vengeance bids against his foes. Our foes
The Pandavas, are furious, treacherous, base,
Halting at nothing; and how say the wise
In holy Shasters? - "Wounded, wearied, fed,
Or fasting - sleeping, waking, setting forth,
Or new arriving; slay thine enemies!"
And so again: "At midnight, when they sleep;
Dawn, when they watch noon, if their leaders fall
Eve, should they scatter all the times and hours
Are times and hours good for killing foes."'
So did the son of Drona steel his soul
To break upon the sleeping Pandu chiefs

And slay them in the darkness. Being set
On this unlordly deed, and clear in scheme,
He from their slumbers roused the warriors twain,
Kripa and Kritavarman."

THE GREAT JOURNEY

To Narayen, lord of lords, be glory given,
To sweet Saraswati, the Queen in heaven
To great Vyâsa, eke, pay reverence due,
That this high story may its course pursue.

THEN Janmejaya prayed: "O Singer, say,
What wrought the princes of the Pandavas
On tidings of the battle so ensued,
And Krishna, gone on high?"

Answered the Sage:
"On tidings of the wreck of Vrishni's race,
King Yudhisthira of the Pandavas
Was minded to be done with earthly things,
And to Arjuna spake: 'O noble Prince,
Time endeth all; we linger, noose on neck,
Till the last day tightens the line, and kills.
Let us go forth to die, being yet alive.'
And Kunti's son, the great Arjuna, said:
'Let us go forth to die! - Time slayeth all.
We will find Death, who seeketh other men.'
And Bhimaseria, hearing, answered: 'Yea,
We will find Death!' and Sahadev cried: 'Yea!'
And his twin brother Nakula; whereat
The princes set their faces for the Mount.

"But Yudhisthira -ere he left his realm
To seek high ending -summoned Yuyutsu,
Surnamed of fights, and set him over all,
Regent, to rule in Parikshita's name
Nearest the throne; and Parikshita, King
He crowned, and unto old Subhadra said:
'This, thy son's son, shall wear the Kuru crown,
And Yadu's offspring, Vajra, shall be first

In Yadu's house. Bring up the little prince
Here in our Hastinpur, but Vajra keep
At Indraprasth; and let it be thy last
Of virtuous works to guard the lads,' and guide.'

"So ordering ere he went, the righteous King
Made offering of white water, heedfully,
To Vasudev, to Rama, and the rest, -
All funeral rites performing; next he spread
A funeral feast, whereat there sat as guests
Narada, Dwaipayana, Bharadwaj,
And Markandeya, rich in saintly years,
And Yajnavalkya, Hari, and the priests
Those holy ones he fed with dainty meats
In kingliest wise, naming the name of Him
'Who bears the bow; and -that it should be well
For him and his -gave to the Brahmanas
Jewels of gold and silver, lakhs on lakhs,
Fair broidered cloths, gardens and villages,
Chariots and steeds and slaves.

"Which being done,
O Best of Bhârat's line he bowed him low
Before his Guru's feet, -at Kripa's feet,
That sage all honored, - saying, 'Take my Prince;
Teach Parikshita as thou taughtest me.
For hearken, ministers and men of war!
Fixed is my mind to quit all earthly state.'
Full sore of heart were they, and sore the folk,
To hear such speech, and bitter went the word
Through town and country, that the King would go;
And all the people cried, 'Stay with us, Lord!'
But Vudhisthira knew his time was come,
Knew that life passes and that virtue lasts,
And put aside their love.

"So, with farewells
Tenderly took of lieges and of lords,
Girt he for travel, with his princely kin,
Great Yudhisthira, Dharma's royal son.

Crest-gem and belt and ornaments he stripped
From off his body, and for broidered robe
A rough dress donned, woven of jungle-bark;
And what he did - O Lord of men!- so did
Arjuna, Bhima, and the twin-bom pair,
Nakula with Sahadev, and she, -in grace
The peerless, - Draupadí. Lastly these six, -
Thou son of Bhârata! - in solemn form
Made the high sacrifice of Naishtiki,
Quenching their flames in water at the close;
And so set forth, midst wailing of all folk
And tears of women, weeping most to see
The Princess Draupadí - that lovely prize
Of the great gaming, Draupadí the Bright -
Journeying afoot; but she and all the five
Rejoiced, because their way lay heavenwards.

"Seven were they, setting forth, - Princess and King,
The King's four brothers, and a faithful dog.
Those left Hastinapur; but many a man,
And all the palace household, followed them
The first sad stage: and, ofttimes prayed to part,
Put parting off for love and pity, still
Sighing, 'A little farther!' - till day waned;
Then one by one they turned, and Kripa said:
'Let all turn back, Yuyutsu! These must go.'
So came they homewards, but the Snake-King's child,
Ulupi, leapt in Gunga, losing them;
And Chitrangâda with his people went
Mournful to Munipoor, whilst those three queens
Brought Parikshita, in.

"Thus wended they,
Pandu's five sons and loveliest Draupadí,
Tasting no meat, and journeying due east,
On righteousness their high hearts fed, to heaven
Their souls assigned; and steadfast trod their feet
By faith upborne - past nullah, ran, and wood,
River and jheel and plain. King Yudhisthir
Walked foremost, Bhima followed, after him

Arjuna, and the twin-born brethren next,
Nakula with Sahadev: in whose still steps-
O Best of Bhârat's offspring! - Draupadí,
That gem of women, paced, with soft, dark face, -
Beautiful, wonderful! -and lustrous eyes,
Clear-edged like lotus-petals; last the dog
Following the Pandavas.

"At length they reach
The far Lauchityan Sea, which foameth white
Under Udayachala's ridge. - Know ye,
That all this while Nakula had not ceased
Bearing the holy bow, named Gandiva,
And jewelled quiver, ever filled with shafts,
Though one should shoot a thousand thousand times.
Here - broad across their path - the heroes see
Agni, the god. As though a mighty hill
Took form of front and breast and limb, he spake.
Seven streams of shining splendor rayed his brow,
While the dread voice said: 'I am Agni, chiefs!
O sons of Pandu, I am Agni! Hail!
O long-armed Yudhisthira, blameless king, -
O warlike Bhima, - O Arjuna, wise, -
O brothers twin-born from a womb divine, -
Hear! I am Agni, who consumed the wood
By will of Narayan for Arjuna's sake.
Let this your brother give Gandiva back,
The matchless bow: the use for it is o'er.
That gem-ringed battle-discus which he hurled
Cometh again to Krishna in his hand
For avatars to be; but need is none
Henceforth of this most excellent bright bow,
Gandiva, which I brought for Partha's aid
From high Varuna. Let it be returned.
Cast it herein!'

"And all the princes said,
"Cast it, dear brother!' So Arjuna threw
Into that sea the quiver ever-filled,
And glittering bow; then, led by Agni's light,

Unto the south they tumed, and so southwest,
And afterwards right west, until they saw
Dwaraka, washed and bounded by a main
Loud -thundering on its shores; and here - O Best
Vanished the god; while yet those heroes walked,
Now to the northwest bending, where long coasts
Shut in the sea of salt, now to the north,
Accomplishing all quarters, journeyed they;
The earth their altar of high sacrifice,
Which these most patient feet did pace around
Till Meru rose.

"At last it rose! These Six,
Their senses subjugate, their spirits pure,
Wending along, came into sight - far off
In the eastern. sky -of awful Himavat;
And, midway in the peaks of Himavat,
Meru, the mountain of all mountains, rose,
Whose head is heaven; and under Himavat
Glared a wide waste of sand, dreadful as death.
"Then, as they hastened o'er the deathly waste,
Aiming for Meru, having thoughts at soul
Infinite, eager, - lo! Draupadí reeled,
With faltering heart and feet - and Bhima turned,
Gazing upon her; aad that hero spake
To Yudhisthira: 'Master, Brother, King!
Why doth she fail? For never all her life
Wrought our sweet lady one thing wrong, I think.
Thou knowest; make us know, why hath she failed?'

"Then Yudhisthira, answered: 'Yea, one thing.
She loved our brothers better than all else, -
Better than heaven: that was her tender sin,
Fault of a faultless soul; she pays for that.'

"So spake the monarch, turning not his eyes,
Though Draupadí lay dead, - striding straight on
For Meru, heart-fall of the things of heaven,
Perfect and firm. But yet a little space
And Sahadev fell down; which Bhima seeing,

Cried once again: 'O King, great Madri's son
Stumbles and sinks. Why hath he sunk? - so true,
So brave and steadfast, and so free from pride!'

"'He was not free,' with countenance still fixed,
Quoth Yudhisthira; 'he was true and fast
And wise; yet wisdom made him proud; he hid
One little hurt of soul, but now it kills.'

"So saying, he strode on, Kunti's strong son,
And Bhima; and Arjuna followed him,
And Nakula, and the hound; leaving behind
Sahadev in the sands. But Nakula,
Weakened and grieved to see Sahadev fall-
His dear-loved brother -lagged and stayed; and then
Prone on his face he fell, that noble face
Which had no match for beauty in the land,
Glorious and godlike Nakula! Then sighed
Bhima anew: 'Brother and Lord! the man
Who never erred from virtue, never broke
Our fellowship, and never in the world
Was matched for goodly perfectness of form
Or gracious feature, - Nakula has fallen!'

"But Yudhisthira, holding fixed his eyes.
That changeless, faithful, king, -replied
'Yea, but he erred! The Godlike form he wore
Beguiled him to believe none like to him,
And he alone desirable, and things
Unlovely, to be slighted. Self-love slays
Our noble brother. Bhima, follow! Each
Pays what his debt was.'

"Which Arjuna heard,
Weeping to see them fall; and that stout son
Of Pandu, that destroyer of his foes,
That Prince, who drove through crimson waves of war,
In old days, with his milk-white chariot-steeds,
He, the arch-hero, sank! Beholding this, -
The yielding of that soul unconquerable,

Fearless, divine, from Sakra's self derived,
Arjuna's, - Bhima cried aloud: 'O King!
This man was surely perfect. Never once,
Not even in slumber, when the lips are loosed,
Spake he one word that was not true as truth.
Ah, heart of gold! why art thou broke? O King!
Whence falleth he?'

"And Yudhisthira said,
Not pausing: 'Once he lied, a lordly lie!
He bragged - our brother - that a single day
Should see him utterly consume, alone,
All those his enemies, -which could not be.
Yet from a great heart sprang the unmeasured speech,
Howbeit a finished hero should not shame
Himself in such wise, nor his enemy,
If he will faultless fight and blameless die
This was Arjuna's sin. Follow thou me!'

"So the King still went on. Put Bhima next
Fainted, and stayed upon the way, and sank ,
But, sinking, cried behind the steadfast Prince:
'Ah, brother, see I die! Look upon me,
Thy well-beloved! Wherefore falter I,
Who strove to stand?'

"And Yudhisthira said:
More than was well the goodly things of earth
Pleased thee, my pleasant brother! Light the offence,
And large thy spirit - but the o'erfed soul
Plumed itself over others. Pritha's son,
For this thou failest, who so near didst gain.'

"Thenceforth alone the long-armed monarch strode,
Not looking back, - nay, not for Bhima's sake,
But walking with his face set for the Mount;
And the hound followed him, - only the hound.

"After the deathly sands, the Mount! and, lo
Sákra shone forth, - the God, - filling the earth

And heavens with thunder of his chariot-wheels.
'Ascend,' he said, I with me, Pritha's great son!
But Yudhisthira answered, sore at heart
For those his kinsfolk, fallen on the way:
O Thousand-eyed, O Lord of all the gods,
Give that my brothers come with me, who fell!
Not without them is Swarga sweet to me.
She too, the dear and kind and queenly, - she
Whose perfect virtue Paradise must crown, -
Grant her to come with us! Dost thou grant this?'

"The God replied: 'In heaven thou shalt see
Thy kinsmen and the Queen - these will attain
And Krishna. Grieve no longer for thy dead,
Thou chief of men I their mortal covering stripped,
These have their places; but to thee the gods
Allot an unknown grace: thou shalt go up,
Living and in thy form, to the immortal homes.'

"But the King answered: 'O thou Wisest One,
Who know'st what was, and is, and is to be,
Still one more grace! This hound hath ate with me,
Followed me, loved me; must I leave him now?'

"'Monarch,' spake Indra, I thou art now as we,
Deathless, divine; thou art become a god;
Glory and power and gifts celestial,
And all the joys of heaven are thine for aye
What hath a beast with these? Leave here thy hound.'

"Yet Yudhisthira answered: 'O Most High,
O Thousand-eyed and wisest! can it be
That one exalted should seem pitiless?
Nay, let me lose such glory: for its sake
I cannot leave one living thing I loved.'

"Then sternly Indra spake: 'He is unclean,
And into Swarga such shall enter not.
The Krodhavasha's wrath destroys the fruits
Of sacrifice, if dogs defile the fire.

Bethink thee, Dharmaraj; quit now this beast
That which is seemly is not hard of heart.'

"Still he replied: ' 'Tis written that to spurn
A suppliant equals in offence to slay
A twice-born; wherefore, not for Swarga's bliss
Quit I, Mahendra, this poor clinging dog,
So without any hope or friend save me,
So wistful, fawning for my faithfulness
So agonized to die, unless I help
Who among men was called steadfast and just.'

"Quoth Indra: 'Nay, the altar-flame is foul
Where a dog passeth; angry angels sweep
The ascending smoke aside, and all the fruits
Of offering, and the merit of the prayer
Of him whom a hound toucheth. Leave it here!
He that will enter heaven must enter pure.
Why didst thou quit thy brethren on the way,
And Krishna, and the dear-loved Draupadî,
Attaining, firm and glorious, to this Mount
Through perfect deeds, to linger for a brute?
Hath Yudhisthira vanquished self, to melt
With one poor passion at the door of bliss?
Stay'st thou for this, who didst not stay for them, -
Draupadí, Bhima?'

"But the King yet spake:
"Tis known that none can hurt or help the dead.
They, the delightful ones, who sank and died,
Following my footsteps, could not live again
Though I had turned, - therefore I did not turn
But could help profit, I had stayed to help.
There be four sins, O Sákra, grievous sins
The first is making suppliants despair,
The second is to slay a nursing wife,
The third is spoiling Brahmans' goods by force,
The fourth is injuring an ancient friend.
These four I deem not direr than the crime,
If one, in coming forth from woe to weal,

Abandon any meanest comrade then.'

"Straight as he spake, brightly great Indra smiled
Vanished the hound, and in its stead stood there
The Lord of Death and justice, Dharma's self!
Sweet were the words which fell from those dread lips,
Precious the lovely praise: 'O thou true King,
Thou that dost bring to harvest the good seed
Of Pandu's righteousness; thou that hast ruth
As he before, on all which lives! - O Son!
I tried thee in the Dwaita wood, what time
They smote thy brothers, bringing water; then
Thou prayed'st for Nakula's life - tender and just -
Nor Bhima's nor Arjuna's, true to both,
To Madri as to Kunti, to both queens,[1]
Hear thou my word! Because thou didst not mount
This car divine, lest the poor hound be shent
Who looked to thee, lo! there is none in heaven
Shall sit above thee, King! - Bhârata's son
Enter thou now to the eternal joys,
Living and in thy form. justice and Love
Welcome thee, Monarch! thou shalt throne with us!'

"Thereat those mightiest gods, in glorious train,
Mahendra, Dharma, - with bright retinue

Of Maruts, Saints, Aswin-Kumâras, Nats
Spirits, and angels bore the King aloft,
The thundering chariot first, and after it
Those airy-moving Presences. Serene,
Clad in great glory, potent, wonderful,
They glide at will, - at will they know and see,
At wish their wills are wrought; for these are pure
Passionless, hallowed, perfect, free of earth.
In such celestial midst the Kuru king
Soared upward, and a sweet light filled the sky.
And fell on earth, cast by his face and form,

---

[1] A reference to the concluding part of "The Enchanted Lake will explain this.

Transfigured as he rose and there was heard
The voice of Narad, - it is he who sings,
Sitting in heaven, the deeds that good men do
In all the quarters, - Narad, chief of bards,
Narad the wise, who laudeth purity, -
So cried he: 'Thou art risen, Kuru king!
Whose greatness is above all royal saints.
Hail, son of Pandu! like to thee is none
Now or before among the sons of men,
Whose fame hath filled the three wide worlds, who corn's
Bearing thy mortal body, which doth shine
With radiance as a god's.'

"The glad King heard
Narad's loud praise; he saw the immortal gods, -
Dharina, Mahendra and dead chiefs and saints,
Known upon earth, in blessèd heaven he saw,
But only those. 'I do desire,' he said,
'That region, be it of the Blest as this,
Or of the Sorrowful some otherwhere,
Where my dcar brothers are, and Draupadí.
I cannot stay elsewhere! I see them not!'

"Then answer made Purandará, the God:
O thou compassionate and noblest one,
Rest in the pleasures which thy deeds have gained.
How, being as are the gods, canst thou live bound
By mortal chains? Thou art become of us,
Who live above hatred and love, in bliss
Pinnacled, safe, supreme. Sun of thy race,
Thy brothers cannot reach where thou hast climbed
Most glorious lord of men, let not thy peace
Be touched by stir of earth! Look! this is heaven.
See where the saints sit, and the happy souls,
Siddhas and angels, and the gods who live
Forever and forever.'

"'King of gods,'
Spake Vudhisthira, I but I will not live
A little space without those souls I loved.

O Slayer of the demons! let me go
Where Bhima and my brothers are, and she,
My Draupadí, the Princess with the face
Softer and darker than the Vrihat-leaf,
And soul as sweet as are its odors. Lo!
Where they have gone, there will I surely go.'"[1]

---

[1] Contrast this magnificent unselfishness with Dante or St. Thomas Aquinas! The Sanskrit text has a noble simplicity, - Gantum ichchami tatra aham yatra mê bhrataro gata.

THE ENTRY INTO HEAVEN

II.

(FROM THE SANSKRIT OF THE SWARGÂROHANA PARVA OF THE MAHÂBHÂRATA.-VOL. IV. OF THF CALCUTTA QUARTO EDITION.)

To Narayen, Lord of lords, be glory given,
To Queen Saraswati be praise in heaven;
Unto Vyâsa pay the reverence due,
So may this story its high course pursue.

THEN Janmejaya said: "I am fain to learn
How it befell with my great forefathers,
The Pandu chiefs and Dhritirashtra's sons,
Being to heaven ascended. If thou know'st,-
And thou know'st all, whom wise Vyâsa taught,
'Fell me, how fared with those mighty souls?"

Answercd the Sage: "Hear of thy forefathers
Great Yudhisthira and the Pandu lords -
How it befell. When thus the blameless King
Was as entered into heaven, there he beheld
Duryodhana, his foe, throned as a god
Amid the gods; splendidly sat that Prince,
Peaceful and proud, the radiance of his brows
Far-shining like the sun's; and round him thronged
Spirits of light, with Sâdhyas, - companies
Goodly to see. But when the King beheld
Duryodhana in bliss, and not his own, -
Not Draupadí, nor Bhima, nor the rest, -
With quick-averted face and angry eyes
The monarch spake: 'Keep heaven for such as these,
If these come here! I do not wish to dwell
Where he is, whom I hated rightfully,
Being a covetous and witless Prince .-

Whose deed it was that in wild fields of war
Brothers and friends by mutual slaughter fell,
While our swords smote, sharpened so wrathfully
By all those wrongs borne wandering in the woods
But Draupadí's the deepest wrong, for he -
He who sits there - haled her before the court,
Seizing that sweet and virtuous lady - he! -
With grievous hand wound in her tresses. Gods,
I cannot look upon him! Sith 'tis so,
Where are my brothers? Thither will I go!'

"Smiling, bright Narada the Saint replied:
'Speak thou not rashly! Say not this, O King!
Those who come here lay enmities aside.
O Yudhisthira, long-armed monarch, hear
Duryodhana is cleansed of sin; he sits
Worshipful as the saints, worshipped by saints
And kings who lived and died in virtue's path,
Attaining to the joys which heroes gain
Who yield their breath in battle. Even so
He that did wrong thee, knowing not thy worth,
Hath won before thee hither, raised to bliss
For lordliness, and valor free of fear.
Ah, well-beloved son! ponder thou not
The memory of that gaming, nor the griefs
Of Draupadí, nor any vanished hurt
Wrought in the passing shows of life by craft
Or wasteful war. Throne happy at the side
Of this thy happy foeman, -wiser now;
For here is Paradise, thou Chief of men
And in its holy air hatreds are dead.'

"Thus by the Saint addressed, the Kuru King
Answered uncomforted: 'Duryodhana,
If he attains, attains; yet not the less
Evil he lived and ill he died, - a heart
Impious and harmful, bringing woes to all,
To friends and foes. His was the crime which cost
Our land its warriors, horses, elephants;
His the black sin that set us in the field,

Burning for rightful vengeance. Ye are gods,
And just; and ye have granted heaven to him.
Show me the regions, therefore, where they dwell,
My brothers, those, the noble-souled, the loyal,
Who kept the sacred laws, who swerved no step
From virtue's path, who spake the truth, and lived
Foremost of warriors. Where is Kunti's son,
The hero-hearted Karna? Where are gone
Sátyaki, Dhrishtadyumna, with their sons?
And where those famous chiefs who fought for me,
Dying a splendid death? I see them not.
O Narada, I see them not! No King
Draupada! no Viráta! no glad face
Of Dhrishtaketu! no Shikandina,
Prince of Panchála, nor his princely boys
Nor Abhimanyu the unconquerable!
President Gods of heaven! I see not here
Radha's bright son, nor Yudhamanyu,
Nor Uttamanjaso, his brother dear!
Where are those noble Maharashtra lords,
Rajas and rajpoots, slain for love of us?
Dwell they in glory elsewhere, not yet seen?
If they be here, high Gods, and those with them
For whose sweet sakes I lived, here will I live,
Meek-hearted; but if such be not adjudged
Worthy, I am not worthy, nor my soul
Willing to rest without them. Ah, I burn,
Now, in glad heaven, with grief, bethinking me
Of those my mother's words, what time I poured
Death-water for my dead at Kurkshetra, -
"Pour for Prince Karna, Son!" but I wist not
His feet were as my mother's feet, his blood
Her blood, my blood. O Gods! I did not know,
Albeit Sákra's self had failed to break
The battle, where he stood. I crave to see
Surya's child, that glorious chief who fell
By Saryasáchi's hand, unknown of me;
And Bhima! ah, my Bhima! dearer far
Than life to me; Arjuna, like a god,
Nakula and Sahadev, twin lords of war,

With tenderest Draupadí! Show me those souls
I cannot tarry where I have them not.
Bliss is not blissful, just and mighty Ones!
Save if I rest beside them. Heaven is there
Where Love and Faith make heaven. Let me go!'

"And answer made the hearkening heavenly Ones:
'Go, if it seemeth good to thee, dear son!
The King of gods commands we do thy will.'

"So saying," the Sage went on, "Dharma's own voice
Gave ordinance, and from the shining bands
A golden Deva glided, taking hest
To guide the King there where his kinsmen were.
So wended these, the holy angel first,
And in his steps the King, close following.
Together passed they through the gates of pearl,
Together heard them close; then to the left
Descending, by a path evil and dark,
Hard to be traversed, rugged,- entered they
The 'SINNERS' ROAD.' The tread of sinful feet
Matted the thick thorns carpeting its slope!
The smell of sin hung foul on them; the mire
About their roots was trampled filth of flesh
Horrid with rottenness, and splashed with gore
Curdling in crimson puddles - where there buzzed
And sucked, and settled, creatures of the swamp,
Hideous in wing and sting, gnat-clouds and flies,
With moths, toads, newts, and snakes red-gulleted
And livid, loathsome worms, writhing in slime
Forth from skull-holes and scalps and tumbled bones.
A burning forest shut the roadside in
On either hand, and 'mid its crackling boughs
Perched ghastly birds, or flapped amidst the flames,-
Vultures and kites and crows, - with brazen plumes
And beaks of iron; and these grisly fowl
Screamed to the shrieks of Prets, - lean, famished ghosts,
Featureless, eyeless, having pin-point mouths,
Hungering, but hard to fill, - all swooping down
To gorge upon the meat of wicked ones;

Whereof the limbs disparted, trunks and heads,
Offal and marrow, littered all the way.
By such a path the King passed, sore afeared
If he had known of fear, for the air stank
With carrion stench, sickly to breathe - and lo
Presently 'thwart the pathway foamed a flood
Of boiling waves, rolling down corpses. This
They passed, and then the Asipatra wood
Spread black in sight, whereof the undergrowth
Was sword-blades, every blade spitting some wretch;
All around poison-trees; and next to this,
Strewn deep with fiery sands, an awful waste,
Wherethrough the wicked toiled with blistering feet,
'Midst rocks of brass, red hot, which scorched, and pools
Of bubbling pitch that gulfed them. Last the gorge
Of Kutashála Mali, - frightful gate
Of utmost Hell, with utmost horrors filled.
Deadly and nameless were the plagues seen there
Which when the monarch reached, nigh overborne
By terrors and the reek of tortured flesh,
Unto the angel spake he: 'Whither goes
This hateful road, and where be they I seek,
Yet find not?' Answer made the heavenly One
'Hither, great King, it was commanded me
To bring thy steps. If 'thou be'st overborne,
It is commanded that I lead thee back
To where the gods wait. Wilt thou turn and mount?'

Then (O thou Son of Bhârat!) Yudhisthir
Turned heavenward his face, so was he moved
With horror and the hanging stench, and spent
By toil of that black travel. Put his feet
Scarce one stride measured, when about the place
Pitiful accents rang: 'Alas, sweet King! -
Ah, saintly Lord! - Ah, thou that hast attained
Place with the Blessed, Pandu's offspring! -pause
A little while for love of us who cry!
Nought can harm thee in all this baneful place
But at thy coming there 'gan blow a breeze
Balmy and soothing, bringing us relief.

O Pritha's son, mightiest of men! we breathe
Glad breath again to see thee; we have peace
One moment in our agonies. Stay here
One moment more, Bhârata's child! Go not,
Thou glory of the Kurus! Being here,
Hell softens and our bitter pains relax.'

"These pleadings, wailing all around the place,
Heard the King Yudhisthira, - words of woe
Humble and eager! and compassion seized
His lordly mind. 'Poor souls unknown!' he sighed,
And hellwards turned anew - for what those were,
Whence such beseeching voices, and of whom,
That son of Pandu wist not, - only wist
That all the noxious murk was filled with forms,
Shadowy, in anguish, crying grace of him.
Wherefore he called aloud: 'Who speaks with me?
What do ye here, and what things suffer ye?'
Then from the black depth piteously there came
Answers of whispered suffering: 'Karna I,
O King!' and yet another: 'O my liege,
Thy Bhima speaks!' and then a voice again:
I am Arjuna, Brother!' and again:
Nakula is here, and Sahadev!' and last,
A moan of music from the darkness sighed:
'Draupadí cries to thee!' Thereat broke forth
The monarch's spirit, knowing so the sound
Of each familiar voice: 'What doom is this?
What have my well-belovèd wrought to earn
Death with the damned, or life loathlier than death
In Narak's midst? Hath Karna erred so deep,
Bhima, Arjuna, or the glorious twins,
Or she, the slender-waisted, sweetest, best,
My Princess, - that Duryodhana should sit
Peaceful in Paradise with all his crew,
Throned by Mahendra and the shining gods?
How should these fail of bliss, and he attain?
What were their sins to his, their splendid faults?
For if they slipped, it was in virtue's way
Serving good laws, performing holy rites,

Boundless in gifts and faithful to the death.
These be their well-known voices! Are ye here,
Souls I loved best? Dream I, belike, asleep,
Or rave I, maddened with accursèd sights,
And death-reeks of this hellish air?

"Thereat
For pity and for pain the King waxed wroth.
That soul fear could not shake, nor trials tire,
Burned terrible with tenderness, the while
His eyes searched all the gloom, his planted feet
Stood fast in the mid horrors. Well-nigh, then,
He cursed the gods; well-nigh that steadfast mind
Broke from its faith in virtue. But he stayed
Th' indignant passion, softly speaking this
Unto the angel: 'Go to those thou serv'st;
Tell them I come not thither. Say I stand
Here in the throat of hell, and here will bide-
Nay, if I perish - while my well-belov'd
Win ease and peace by any pains of mine.'

"Whereupon, nought replied the shining One,
But straight repaired into the upper light,
Where Sákra sat above the gods, and spake
Before the gods the message of the King."

"AFTERWARDS, What befell? the Prince inquired.
"Afterwards, Princely One replied the Sage,
"At hearing and at knowing that high deed
(Great Yudhisthira braving hell for love),
The Presences of Paradise uprose,
Each Splendor in his place, - God Sákra chief:
Together rose they and together stepped
Down from their thrones, treading the nether road
Where Yudhisthira tarried. Sákra led
The shining van, and Dharma, Lord of laws,
Paced glorious next. O Son of Bhárata,
While that celestial company came down-
Pure as the white stars sweeping through the sky,
And brighter than their brilliance - look! hell's shades

Melted before them; warm gleams drowned the gloom
Soft, lovely scenes rolled over the ill sights;
Peace calmed the cries of torment; in its bed
The boiling river shrank, quiet and clear;
The Asipatra Vana - awful wood -
Blossomed with colors; all those cruel blades,
And dreadful rocks, and piteous scattered wreck
Of writhing bodies, where the King had passed,
Vanished as dreams fade. Cool and fragrant went
A wind before their faces, as these gods
Drew radiant to the presence of the King,
Maruts; and Vasus eight, who shine and serve
Round Indra; Rudras; Aswins; and those Six
Immortal Lords of light beyond our light.
Th' Adityas; Saddhyas - Siddhas, -these were there,
With angels, saints, and habitants of heaven,
Smiling resplendent round the steadfast Prince.

"Then spake the God of gods these gracious words
To Yudhisthira, standing in that place:-
"'King Yudhisthira! O thou long-armed Lord,
This is enough! All Heaven is glad of thee.
It is enough! Come, thou most blessed one,
Unto thy peace, well-gained. Lay here aside
Thy loving wrath, and hear the speech of Heaven.
It is appointed that all kings see hell.
The reckonings for the life of men are twain:
Of each man's righteous deeds a tally true,
A tally true of each man's evil deeds.
Who hath wrought little right, to him is paid
A little bliss in Swarga, then the woe
Which purges; who much right hath wrought, from him
The little ill by lighter pains is cleansed,
And then the joys. Sweet is peace after pain,
And bitter pain which follows peace: yet they
Who sorely sin taste of the heaven they miss,
And they that suffer quit their debt at last.
Lo! We have loved thee, laying hard on thee
Grievous assaults of soul, and this black road.
Bethink thee: by a semblance once, dear Son!

Drona thou didst beguile; and once, dear Son!
Semblance of hell hath so thy sin assoiled,
Which passeth with these shadows. Even thus
Thy Bhima came a little space t' account,
Draupadí, Krishna, - all whom thou didst love,
Never again to lose! Come, First of men!
These be delivered and their quittance made.
Also the Princes, son of Bhárata!
Who fell beside thee fighting, have attained.
Come thou to see! Karna, whom thou didst mourn,-
That mightiest archer, master in all wars, -
He hath attained, shining as doth the sun;
Come thou and see! Grieve no more, King of men!
Whose love holped them and thee, and hath its meed.
Rajas and maharajas, warriors, aids, -
All thine are thine forever. Krishna waits
To greet thee coming, 'companied by gods,
Seated in heaven, from toils and sorrows saved.
Son! there is golden fruit of noble deeds,
Of prayer, alms, sacrifice. The most just gods
Keep thee thy place above the highest saints,
Where thou shalt sit, divine, compassed about
With royal souls in bliss, as Hari sits;
Seeing Mándháta crowned, and Bhagirath,
Daushyanti, Bhârata, with all thy line.
Now therefore wash thee in this holy stream,
Gunga's pure fount, whereof the bright waves bless
All the Three Worlds. It will so change thy flesh
To likeness of th' immortal, thou shalt leave
Passions and aches and tears behind thee there.'

"And when the awful Sákra thus had said,
Lo Dharma spake, - th' embodied Lord of Right:-

"Bho! bho! I am well pleased! Hail to thee, Chief
Worthy, and wise, and firm. Thy faith is full,
Thy virtue, and thy patience, and thy truth,
And thy self mastery. Thrice I put thee, King!
Unto the trial, In the Dwaita wood,
The day of tempting, -then thou stoodest fast

Next. on thy brethren's death and Draupadí's,
When, as a dog, I followed thee, and found
Thy sprit constant to the meanest friend.
Here was the third and sorest touchstone, Son!
That thou shouldst hear thy brothers cry in hell,
And yet abide to help them. Pritha's child,
We love thee! Thou art fortunate and pure,
Past trials now. Thou art approved, and they
Thou lov'st have tasted hell only a space,
Not meriting to suffer more than when
An evil dream doth come, and Indra's beam
Ends it with radiance, - as this vision ends.
It is appointed that all flesh see death,
And therefore thou hast borne the passing pangs,
Briefest for thee, and brief for those of thine,
Bhima the faithful, and the valiant twins
Nakula and Sahadev, and those great hearts
Karna, Arjuna, with thy princess dear,
Draupadí. Come, thou best-belovèd Son,
Blessed of all thy line! Bathe in this stream,
It is great Gunga, flowing through Three Worlds.'

"Thus high-accosted, the rejoicing King
(Thy ancestor, O Liege!) proceeded straight
Unto that river's brink, which floweth pure
Through the Three Worlds, mighty, and sweet, and praised,
There, being bathed, the body of the King
Put off its mortal, coming up arrayed
In grace celestial, washed from soils of sin,
From passion, pain, and change. So, hand in hand
With brother-gods, glorious went Yudhisthir,
Lauded by lovely minstrelsy, and songs
Of unknown music, where those heroes stood -
The princes of the Pandavas, his kin
And lotus-eyed and loveliest Draupadí,
Waiting to greet him, gladdening and glad."